BEWARE THE SHILL

ALSO BY JOHN SHEPPHIRD

The Shill
Kill the Shill

JOHN SHEPPHIRD

BEWARE THE SHILL

A Tale of Deception

DOWN & OUT BOOKS

Down & Out Books Edition: August 2016

Down & Out Books
3959 Van Dyke Rd, Ste. 265
Lutz, FL 33558
www.DownAndOutBooks.com

Cover by Ricardo Netro

ISBN: 1-943402-36-1
ISBN-13: 978-1-943402-36-6

For Jennifer

CHAPTER 1

Jane could feel the stitches on her leg tear. Blood streamed but she pushed through the pain, running for her life. She looked back, couldn't see him—wasn't sure if he was following.

She had just seen a ghost.

Only moments ago Cooper had surprised her. The man she thought was dead asked her to help him kill Veronica. She had said, "I won't be an accomplice to murder."

"I'm not asking you to," he replied.

"Sounds like you are."

Since the day she'd identified Cooper's corpse she couldn't get the image of his rotted face and shriveled hands out of her mind. But that was his brother, a mistaken identity, and now here Cooper was, alive, the lover that betrayed her—Jane's partner in crime.

"You lied to me," she'd said. "You set me up. Why would I help you?"

"Because unless we get to Veronica first, she'll kill you."

That gave Jane pause. She thought about the assassin, who failed to strangle her in the Los Angeles jail; the one hired by Veronica. The same man followed Jane to Florida to finish the job. If it wasn't for the .38 Special under her pillow, and a little bit of luck, she realized she'd be dead. She backed off and tried to distance herself from him.

"She won't stop," he pressed.

"I'll go where she can't find me."

"But she will find you. She'll kill your mother to draw you out," he said.

The thought clinched her heart. Her mother Nancy was the only family she'd ever known—the one person in Jane's life who truly loved her. Cooper added, "We both know who you're dealing with."

To Jane he seemed older and far less handsome than she'd remembered. He was unshaven. His hair was long, and his clothes disheveled. This wasn't the master of the universe she'd fallen in love with. She said to him, "But you and Veronica were lovers at one time."

He nodded, said, "Technically we're still married."

"You're asking me to help you kill the mother of your child?"

"We won't kill her. We'll nail her for good so Billy doesn't grow to become a monster."

She recalled Veronica's boy. He had punched Jane in the nose at his lavish birthday party when Jane was disguised as a clown. He seemed beyond spoiled and a total brat. She said, "So he doesn't become a monster? It's too late for that."

"You have every right to hate me. I had to let you know I'm still alive. I had to warn you."

"Warn me?"

"And ask for your help. We don't have much time."

"I wish I would have never met you," she said. Jane yearned to be the pathetically broke, out-of-work actress once again. Sure she was lonely back in Los Angeles, and miserable, but at least there was peace in her life. At least people weren't trying to kill her.

With regret, he said, "I should have never groomed you to be my shill."

"This is your war, not mine."

"War. That's exactly what it is," he said with a nod. "And you're on the front line."

"Leave me out of it."

"Ever read Sun Tzu?"

"Who?"

"He wrote *The Art of War* in 500 B.C. Do you know what I'm talking about?"

She vaguely knew what he referring to. She'd heard the book mentioned in military shows on Discovery Channel.

"Sun Tzu claims 'All warfare is based on deception,'" Cooper said.

"You're the one who taught me all about deception."

"I suppose, but you were exceptional," he said with a glimmer in his eye.

"I'm just an actress," she said. "It's craft."

"You're much more than that. You're smart and determined. You found Veronica. You cracked her world wide open and she's back on her heels now. But she won't lick her wounds forever. She'll counterattack. That I know."

"What makes you so sure?"

"Because I know her, and I know how she thinks. About the enemy Sun Tzu wrote, 'When we are near, we must make the enemy believe we are far away; when far away, we must make the enemy believe we are near.'" He paused and then continued from memory, "'Hold out baits to entice the enemy.'"

"I won't be your bait," she said with anger.

"You won't be. Realize you're the one person that has stripped virtually everything Veronica owns. You deceived the master of deception. Veronica will avenge."

"Not if she can't find me."

"You've been lucky so far," he said, "but you can't count on luck forever."

"I'll take my chances."

"Listen, Veronica's got one last card to play and I know exactly what it is. She needs money, desperately. When we were together we tried to pull a caper together. The time wasn't right, but now it is. She's finally got the break she's been waiting for, and Veronica's going for gold... literally."

"Fool's gold?"

He laughed. "No. Her plan is to retrieve hidden treasure off the California coast, lost gold from a sunken steamship."

"Is Anne Bonny part of all this?" she asked, remembering that Veronica claimed to be a proud descendant of the notorious female pirate.

"This tragedy at sea was long after Anne Bonny's time."

Jane remembered and said, "I saw Anne Bonny's portrait over her mantle on Stingray Cay."

"Yes. Veronica cherished that."

"What's this tragedy at sea?"

"We discovered it together when Veronica and I were looking to entice suckers into a scheme. She was researching priceless coins from shipwrecks and we came across a treasure map. It checked out, buried gold on government land, impossible to get because it's so heavily guarded."

"Where?" Jane questioned.

"Vandenberg Air Force Base on California's Central Coast. Any day now permission will be granted and she plans to excavate the gold under the guise of scientific study, as if she's leading an expedition, like Jacques Cousteau, saving wildlife under the cloak of animal welfare. We don't have much time."

"Sounds crazy...buried treasure."

"Jane, listen to me," he said, "You and I made a great team, and I need you." Cooper placed a hand on her arm. His physical touch was like a jolt of lightning to her. It sparked a conflict of memories, thoughts both good and bad. "And believe it or not," Cooper continued with a squeeze, "you need me."

She backed off, angered. "Get your hands off of me!"

"Jane, listen I—"

"I don't need anybody. Stay out of my life!" Jane broke into a run. She crossed the six-lane highway, cars swerving to avoid her, blaring horns. When she turned back she couldn't see Cooper.

Where'd he go?

Pain surged from the knife wound Veronica had inflicted, bleeding now, a not-so-gentle reminder of their life-or-death struggle. Jane avoided the Motel 6 she'd stayed in the night before. She cut through a used car lot. She didn't know if Cooper was following, and wondered how he'd found her. Danny's garage was about a mile or so away. Full of fear and adrenaline, she could make there in less than ten minutes.

CHAPTER 2

Jane knew her mom's boyfriend Danny kept a hide-a-key in the planter outside the office door. She entered the business park, slowed to a brisk walk, and found Danny's shop. Still looking back over her shoulder, Cooper was nowhere in sight, so she dug out the hidden key and entered the through the office door.

The stitches on her leg felt prickly now. She could see blood seeping through the gauze bandage as she went for the water cooler to quench her thirst. Jane was gulping from the paper cup when she heard a voice call out, "Jane?"

She spun to see Danny standing beside the trailer. She hadn't noticed the rig when she came in, nor had she seen his truck. "You're back?" she said, surprised.

"We got home late last night. Where were you?" Danny asked, a look of concern on his face.

"I stayed at a motel. Where's Mom?"

"We've been calling you for days, and worried sick," he said, angry. "Your mother insisted we rush back to make sure you're all right."

Jane hadn't filled them in on everything that had happened in the Turks and Caicos. She knew how her mother worried and didn't want to inflict her with anxiety. And then, exhausted from her travels, she'd put her phone on mute and forgot that she'd done that. She hadn't taken her cell phone to Starbucks that morning and realized it was still on her charger on the motel room's bedside table.

"Are you okay?" he asked.

"I couldn't stay home last night."

"A neighbor said police cars were there all day yesterday. What happened?"

"I killed a man," she confessed in a quivering voice, "with your gun." Saying the words made Jane realize the gravity of what she'd done—taken a man's life. Sure it was self-defense, but he was dead.

"Who?"

"He broke into your house and tried to kill me. Veronica's assassin."

"Where's the gun now?" Danny asked.

"The police have it."

"Why didn't you call us?" he asked.

She didn't know why she hadn't called, realized she should have, but so much had happened so fast. Maybe a part of her didn't trust Danny, she thought, or any man for that matter. She wanted to run away and hide. "I'm sorry," Jane said.

Danny's eyes traveled down to her leg, now bleeding below the bandage.

"What happened there?" he asked.

"That's where Veronica stabbed me."

"Where is she?"

"I don't know," she said, tears of frustration filling her eyes.

"Let's get you home."

She handed Danny the hide-a-key back. "I remembered you had this hidden, that's how I got in."

"There's a hide-a-key for the Chevy too," he said. "Under the left fender. Always a good idea to have backup."

"Your car's back at the motel."

"Don't worry about that. We'll get it later."

Less than an hour later Jane was sitting at the dining room table in Danny's suburban home. Her mother tended to Jane's stitches with cotton swabs and a tube of Neosporin. Danny had gone to the Motel 6 to get her things, including her cell phone, and the pillow she'd brought. He now stood at the sliding glass door smoking a cigarette.

Jane told them everything, how she discovered Veronica living in the Turks and Caicos, how she infiltrated the birthday party disguised as a clown, and how former victim Gallagher impersonated an FBI agent only later to storm Veronica's island, fall into a trap, and get himself killed.

Jane explained all the steps she'd taken to survive including her battle in shark-infested waters. She explained how the sharks went after Buddy instead of her, and how she and Veronica battled on the deck of her speeding yacht. Jane explained how the boat ran aground and how Veronica, an experienced swimmer, escaped the wreckage and vanished from the island with her son.

Lastly Jane told them about Cooper. She was certain he was dead before he somehow reappeared at a nearby Starbucks. She feared she was being watched. "We need to hide out," Jane said, "until they can catch Veronica or she'll kill me."

"Oh, Jane," her mother said, "why didn't you call us?"

"I should have, I'm sorry, but it was only yesterday that I got back from the Turks and Caicos. I told the cops what happened and figured they were going to put me in jail. But they didn't. After they left I was alone and got really scared because Veronica knows I live here. She sent that assassin."

"Oh, Jane," her mother said, near tears.

"I went to the Motel 6 where nobody could find me, even you guys, because I just wanted to sleep. But somehow," Jane said, "Cooper tracked me down. He must have been watching the house."

"And the police took my gun?" Danny asked.

"That's right."

Nancy questioned Danny, "Will that be a problem?"

"Hopefully not," he said, drawing on his cigarette and tossing the butt into a Folgers can on the concrete porch.

"You seem concerned," Nancy pressed.

"That .38 Special has the serial number filed off," he said. "So there's a good chance they'll be back to ask me about it."

Jane vaguely remembered a scratch on the face of the pistol below the barrel. She asked, "Where do you get a gun with the serial number filed off?"

"It had the number when I got it," he said softly.

"You filed it off?" Nancy asked.

"Yes."

Jane ventured, "Why?"

Danny and Nancy shared a look. Her mother nodded to him before he confessed, "I didn't buy that snubnose. It was my friend Smitty's and registered in his name. But he's not around anymore and I was afraid if it fell into the wrong hands they'd trace Smitty, through this gun, back to me. Should have thrown that damn thing in Gulf."

Jane said, "Who's Smitty?"

"You're going to have to tell her," Nancy said to Danny.

He considered that for a moment, a somber look on his face.

"Tell me what?" Jane asked.

"She's my daughter, Danny," Nancy said. "And we're your family now."

That surprised Jane. She sat back in the vinyl padded dining room chair. "Are you guys married?"

Nancy held up her hand to show Jane the diamond wedding ring. "Yes, honey, in Las Vegas.

We've been meaning to make the announcement but...it was spontaneous."

Jane didn't know what to say so simply blurted out, "Congratulations."

"We'll have a proper wedding reception," Nancy affirmed. "I promise."

It was Jane's turn to ask, "So why didn't *you* tell *me*?"

"Well...Danny and the team set the track record at the Las Vegas Motor Speedway while we were qualifying for the NHRA Toyota Nationals. We celebrated that night by getting married. Well, maybe we celebrated first," she said with a smile, "and then we got married."

"I'm so happy for you," Jane said, a little hurt that she wasn't invited to at least witness the ceremony. The image of a cheesy Vegas wedding chapel and a gaudy Elvis preacher flashed in her mind. Maybe it was better she wasn't there.

"I'm a lucky man to have met your mother. It's been a long, long time since I've had love in my life. Way too long."

Nancy reached out to him. He stepped over and they held each other's hands, like teenagers. "I've been honest with your mother and I suppose she's right. You have a right to know, especially now that we're family. There was a time when I did a lot of flying, back in the eighties."

"Danny's a pilot," Nancy said.

"*Was* a pilot," he corrected. "I let my license

lapse long ago." He moved from the glass door to the kitchen and poured himself a cup of coffee. "I'm not proud of it, but as a young man I flew special cargo from South America and the Caribbean to the U.S., no questions asked."

Jane shot a look to her mother who gave her a nod.

"My part was to simply land the aircraft and walk away," Danny continued. "In a couple of days I'd get a package delivered to my front door, my fee, in cash. That's how it worked, and that's what I did for many years."

Jane had images of *Miami Vice* with Don Johnson wearing a pastel blazer, mirrored sunglasses, and his sleeves rolled up. She asked, "Cocaine?"

He sipped his coffee. "Mostly that, and sometimes guns from here to there."

"Guns?" Jane asked.

"Weapons delivered to the Contra rebels in Nicaragua," he confessed. "We freelanced for an outfit that became to be known as 'The Enterprise.'"

"What's that?"

"A covert operation run by the National Security Council and the CIA. Oliver North kind of stuff."

Jane vaguely knew what he was talking about from segments she'd seen on TV. The image of Oliver North on the witness stand dressed in full uniform came to mind. It was a part of recent history she knew very little about.

Danny continued, "It was never political for Smitty and me...just a paycheck. We flew under the radar, got really good at skimming the water," he said as he demonstrated with his hand over the Formica table.

Jane looked to her mother.

Nancy nodded and said, "But this was a long time ago."

"Long before I knew your mother," Danny said. "That .38 was registered to Smitty. He'd bought it in San Antonio as a hideaway and kept it in an ankle holster in case things turned melancholy."

"Melancholy?" Jane asked.

Danny nodded. "That's right. We were a great team but then Smitty met a young lady, fell in love, and got married. He had himself a kid and wanted to get out of the business. I'd made enough money by that point, so agreed. It made sense. We'd pushed our luck far enough and it was only a matter of time before we'd crash into the ocean or get caught. But the problem was we were good at what we did. Getting out of the trade is difficult. We tried to break off, but..."

"Things turned melancholy," Jane said.

"Unfortunately, yes. What was supposed to be our last run, on an abandoned tarmac overgrown with weeds, we landed to make a drop. That's when they killed Smitty."

"Who?"

"The Columbians. If it wasn't for that .38 strapped to Smitty's ankle they would have gotten me too."

Intrigued, Jane asked, "What happened?"

"I shot my way out of there. It was a mess. I hid out for years, but that's no way to live, believe me, watching my back the entire time, scared of my own shadow." Danny squeezed Nancy's hand and said, "I found work as a mechanic and that's how I got into the racing business."

"This drug cartel, are they still after you?" Jane asked him.

"It's been so many years...most of those guys are either dead or incarcerated. But the police and FBI don't necessarily let it go. It's complicated."

"FBI?" Jane questioned with Agent Lange coming to her mind.

"They've always suspected I know something about it, which I do." He paused and continued, "That's why I filed the serial number off, so I can't be connected to the carnage of that day."

Jane looked to her mother who said, "We've all made mistakes."

Danny affirmed with a nod. "And I regret it every day. So this going away and hiding...I don't do that anymore. Like I said, it's no way to live."

"You don't understand," Jane tried to explain, "Veronica has incredible connections."

Danny considered that, stood, and with a smile

said, "Come here, darlin'. Let me show you a little something."

Jane stood and followed Danny into the foyer, Nancy behind her. He opened the hall closet and reached for a hidden latch beneath the shelves. A false door revealed a hidden compartment. Jane was shocked to see an assortment of pistols, even a compact machine gun. *Machine gun?* Her jaw dropped.

Danny explained, "Most of these were gifted by some of my former clients."

"The Columbians?" asked Jane.

"Not them. Reagan-era arms dealers I worked for, most of them long gone by now, too." He reached in and pulled down a flat black machine gun pistol. A wire shoulder stock folded into the pistol's handle. "This here is the American made MAC-10, illegal for civilians to own, for obvious reasons."

To Jane, the gun appeared like something Chuck Norris would blow bad guys away in a bad '80s action movie, or maybe Steven Seagal. "Wow," is all she could think to say, hiding her trepidation at the sight of all these weapons.

"If this Veronica decides to send more of her friends..." Danny said, and let it hang there.

CHAPTER 3

Jane couldn't help but peer out the windows of Danny's home. Although she couldn't see Cooper out there, she suspected he had not gone away. She felt he was still watching the house and it made her uneasy.

Meanwhile Danny hid an assortment of guns in drawers and under furniture. He methodically showed both Jane and Nancy where each one was stashed, and later, when Jane was helping her mother make breakfast she asked her, "When did you find out about all of this?"

Nancy made sure Danny was out of earshot before she confessed. "After we'd been with each other for a while, and I'd moved in. He wanted me to know if something happened to him..."

"So," Jane said, "my late father went to prison for writing bad checks." She remembered from what her mother had said. "And now my stepfather worked for the drug cartel and was somehow involved in the Iran-Contra Scandal? You sure know how to pick 'em, Mom."

"When Danny told me about his past, I was naturally cautious, but it was such a long time ago, and we've all made mistakes. With your father, I wasn't oblivious to what he was doing. I'm guilty too, but they didn't throw me in jail, maybe because I was pregnant with you. I was fully aware of what your father was doing," she confessed. "Hell, I think I encouraged him."

"Really?"

"We were so naïve back then. All we cared about was ourselves. It caught up with us. But I believe in second chances, Jane. We learn from our mistakes. I've faltered, so has Danny, and now so have you."

Jane remembered the moment when she visited her mother attending the Pomona Winter Nationals back in California. At the time Jane was in the midst of the scam that started it all, impersonating Cooper's wife, playing the part of a carefree heiress while living in the plush Beverly Hills hotel. That day Nancy revealed that her father wasn't the handsome stranger who rode off into the sunset, what she always thought he was. Instead he had been incarcerated and tragically knifed to death in prison. At the time Jane wondered if her own criminality had been passed down from her father's DNA. Now she learned more about her mother's penchant for larceny. If it was a heritable trait, Jane's fate was in the cards from day one.

Jane wondered aloud, "Can we ever really escape our past, or does it follow us forever?"

"I don't know, honey," Nancy said. "But we can change our ways, and make amends."

The doorbell sounded. Danny entered the living room and somberly said, "Sheriff's here."

Jane and Nancy shared a look.

"Don't say a thing. Let me handle this," he said.

At the door, Jane recognized FBI Agent Lange, plus the pair of Deputy Sheriffs from the day before. These were the two officers that had come to Danny's garage to confirm her whereabouts after she'd been released from jail and moved to Florida. Jane didn't trust them.

Agent Lange made the introductions. He gave Jane a nod and said, "Jane, how are your holding up?"

"Okay," she lied.

"Please let me know if there's anything I can do," he said. There was an edge in his voice and it made her uneasy. Was he an ally or someone to be feared? He held out a color photocopy for Danny, images of a .38 Special. "Mister Dobson, concerning the unfortunate incident at your home the other day," Agent Lange said, "Miss Innes used this weapon to defend herself and claimed she'd gotten it from you."

"That's right," Danny said. "Since she was going to be here alone I showed her where I stashed it."

"Can you tell me where you acquired this weapon?" Agent Lange asked.

"Is there a problem?" Danny returned.

"Well..." Agent Lange looked to Jane before returning his attention to Danny. "It appears the serial number has been filed off."

"I'm aware of that," Danny said deadpan. "That's how it was when I got it."

"And where did you get it?" he asked.

"Gun show, as I recall. It was a long time ago," Danny said.

"The thing is..." Agent Lange said, "according to our lab, the numbers weren't shaved off with a common metal file. It was clearly done in a machine shop, with sophisticated equipment, by a machinist or expert metallurgist. You own a speed shop, am I right?"

"I race top fuel, that's correct."

Agent Lange said, "One can never really shave off a serial number, not on a gun anyway. Through X-ray there's a way to extract the number, and we've done that."

"So what's the problem?" Danny asked.

"It appears this gun was owned by Lyle Smith of Beaumont, Texas."

Danny shot a look to the two sheriffs, then confessed, "Now I remember. I knew Smitty, and I didn't get that pistol from a gun show. He gave it to me after his daughter was born, to get it out of the house and so his wife wouldn't know about it."

"He gifted it to you?"

"Smitty and I were buddies."

"Were?"

"He's dead now," Danny said eyeing Agent Lange. "What's this all about?"

"If you don't mind, I'd like to show you a few more photos, but we don't have them here. Do you mind taking a few minutes out of your day and following us down to the field office here in Sarasota? I promise it won't take long."

Nancy clutched Jane's arm. She could feel her mother's nails dig.

Danny calmly responded with, "Whatever I can do to help."

"Thank you," Agent Lange said, and stepped back.

Danny turned to Nancy. "Honey, turn off the tea kettle for me. I won't be long." With that he crossed the threshold and stepped outside.

CHAPTER 4

"Shit," Nancy said as they watched from the window. Jane could see Danny climb into his pickup, back out of the driveway, and follow the government vehicles before the sheriff's car brought up the rear. "Danny said he knew this day would come," Jane's mother said. "He claims they have a dossier on him, whatever that means."

"This is all my fault," Jane said, feeling horrible.

Nancy bit her lip. "Now what did he say to...?" Then she snapped her finger and marched into the living room. From the bookshelf Nancy pulled down a leather-bound Bible. She thumbed through the pages and a business card fell out. She picked it up from the carpet, tossed the Bible onto Danny's crushed-velvet Barcalounger, and went for the phone.

"Our savior," Nancy said as she punched numbers.

"A pastor?" Jane questioned.

"No, honey. Danny doesn't drink tea, never has. Saying there's a kettle on the stove, that's code to call his lawyer."

"Code?"

"So it wasn't obvious in front of mixed company," her mother said, and then into the phone, "Good morning. Avery Weeks please, it's urgent."

Jane wondered what other secrets her mother and Danny shared.

As instructed, Jane and Nancy waited in the air-conditioned comfort of the Courtyard Marriott, a hotel just around the corner from Sarasota's Sheriff Station. Her mother explained that Danny's lawyer, Avery Weeks, had spent years in the prosecutor's office before he crossed the street to hang his shingle as a criminal defense lawyer.

Nancy had met Avery at his annual Derby Day party, a dressy garden affair where, as Nancy explained, "They serve mint julips in iced pewter mugs to the ladies while the men sip twenty-year-old Pappy."

"What's Pappy?" Jane asked.

"Pappy Van Winkle's a bourbon," her mother explained. "A twenty-year-old bottle is very hard to come by, but not for Avery."

"How's that?"

"Apparently there was some kind of heist of this bourbon years ago, from the Buffalo Trace Distillery in Kentucky. Many pallets of the stuff went missing worth hundreds of thousands of dollars."

"A bourbon heist?" Jane questioned, intrigued by the thought.

"I know it sounds crazy, but Danny suspects one of Avery's clients was involved in this caper, so in lieu of the lawyer fee..."

"Why does Danny suspect that?" Jane asked.

"I don't know. It's just what Danny said. Avery is his insurance policy in case something comes up unexpected."

"Like his past?"

"Please don't judge him. He's a good man. We've all made mistakes."

"He's great. I'm happy for you, Mom. I just feel horrible that I've brought this all upon him."

"We're family. We'll get through this together," she said, a hint of emotion in her tone.

The automatic doors slid opened and a portly middle-aged man made his grand entrance. Jane's first impression was that Avery couldn't be more of a cliché: bow tie, cane, puffy grey sideburns. The only thing missing was a seersucker suit and he could have stepped right out of central casting.

Nancy introduced her daughter.

"It's my pleasure, Miss Innes," he said in a Southern drawl, "and I'm sorry we have to meet under these unfortunate circumstances." As silver-tongued lawyers come, Jane could see Avery was the real deal.

They took a seat in high-back padded chairs in the corner of the lobby and Avery, in his genteel manner, explained, "Ladies, I'm happy to report that I've just spoken with Danny and he is doing just fine. Fortunately he didn't say anything to incriminate himself, but unfortunately it appears they've made an arrest."

"Oh my," Nancy gasped.

"It's merely a formality. I sense they don't have much of a case."

"A case for what?" Jane asked.

Avery looked to Jane and paused before Nancy said, "It's okay. She knows about Danny's past."

Avery nodded, then started in. "Many years ago, at a private airport near Corpus Christi, there was a shootout with a number casualties, including Danny's acquaintance Smitty. Unfortunately an undercover federal agent also perished that day, and since there's no statute of limitations on murder..."

"Why was there a shootout?" Jane asked.

"I'm sure it had something to do with the cargo found in one of the planes."

"And they feel Danny was involved in the killing?" asked Nancy.

"Yes, my dear. Since an undercover agent fell in the line of duty they're compelled to take action." Jane could see her mother's face turn pale. Avery continued, "Fortunately Danny set aside a trust to handle emergencies such as this, and he entrusted me as the executor."

"A what?" Nancy asked.

"A trust, my dear, a fund set aside for a rainy day. He's never had need for my professional services until now and I very much applaud him for his foresight. Luck comes to those prepared. However, because it's Sunday he's going to have to stay overnight, unfortunately, before a judge can set bail for his release."

"Overnight?" Nancy said with concern.

"Tomorrow will come soon enough, and he'll be all right."

"Oh..." Nancy lamented in a worried tone.

"I understand you two were recently married?"

Nancy nodded, "Yes. We've been talking about it for quite some time."

"Congratulations," he said, and then turned to Jane. "Miss Innes, I'm aware of your unfortunate incident, the home invasion in which you were forced to defend yourself..."

"Yes?" Jane said.

"And I understand you're in some sort of a heated dispute."

"I'm in a dispute, all right," Jane said.

"According to Danny," Avery continued, "you feel these hostilities are life threatening. Is that correct?"

Jane thought about what Cooper had said to her, how Veronica would stop at nothing to seek revenge. "Knowing who I've crossed," she said, "I'm concerned."

"And who is it, my dear, that you've crossed?" he asked.

"Veronica Tattinger. Do you know of her?"

He shook his head and said, "Can't say I do."

"Lady Vee?" Jane ventured, using Veronica's nickname from the island. "Does that ring a bell?"

"I am not familiar with that, either," Avery said, stroking his mutton chop sideburns.

"That man who came for me was a hired assassin," Jane explained. "She'll send more, or come herself."

Avery asked, "Is there anything I can do to help?"

"Yes. You can." Jane turned to her mother. "Mom, I can't stay in Florida. I'd be putting you at risk, and looking over my shoulder every minute. I've got to lay low for a while."

"But we're family," Nancy said. "And at times like these we need to stick together."

"Veronica knows all about me, and until she's caught..." Jane turned back to Avery. "Can you help me get a new identity?"

"I'm not one to..." he started in.

"With all due respect, counselor," Jane said, referring to him by his profession to make her point formal, "you're a criminal lawyer and I'm sure you know how do it. Please, set me up with a new identity. You can have it back when Veronica is caught, or dead."

"Dead?" Nancy questioned.

"According to Cooper she'd rather die than rot in jail," Jane said.

"Coming from a man that faked his own death?" Nancy quipped.

Jane ignored her and turned to Avery. "Can you get me a new identity?"

From the look in his eye she knew he could.

CHAPTER 5

Jane and her mother returned home, and although there were an assortment of guns recently planted around the house, Jane still felt insecure. To make matters worse, when she checked her phone Jane saw that Cooper had texted her.

Why did you run? Call me.

Sitting at the dining room table again, Jane echoed her concerns. She told her mother how deeply she felt she needed stay hidden, now more than ever.

"Where will you go?" Nancy asked.

Jane had already thought about it and said, "The semester I spent in college, one of my friends encouraged me to work in dinner theater. She did it, but at the time I thought it was below me because I wanted to act in film and TV roles and needed to be in Los Angeles. But now it makes sense. She's still working there and says there's always need for help."

"Doing what?"

"I'd start by selling tickets and concessions, work as a stage hand, and be available as an understudy. The Wild West Melodrama in Santa Maria, on California's Central Coast." Having driven the area a few years ago, Jane knew Vandenberg Air Force Base was not far from there.

Nancy proposed. "Assuming Avery can spring Danny like he says, we can meet at Sonoma Raceway in Sonoma, California. You can see us race."

There was a knocking noise coming from outside and Jane flinched. She jumped up and darted to the hallway. She tried to remember where the closest gun was stashed.

Nancy remained at the dining room table, asked, "What are you doing?"

"What was that?"

"What?"

"That noise."

"What noise?"

"Outside."

Nancy got up and went to the sliding glass door. She looked out and said, "I didn't hear anything."

"A bump or something," Jane said. "It sounds like someone's out there." She heard the noise again and said, "That!" She recalled there was a pistol under the couch and considered going for it.

Nancy explained, "That's just the air conditioning kicking on."

Jane concentrated on the noise until she realized it was the air conditioning and not a threat. "They know I'm here," she said.

"Who?"

"Veronica. Cooper. I have to leave."

Her mother reluctantly agreed. She made tacos for dinner, a dish Jane always loved as a kid, and they spent the evening on the couch watching TV. Convinced someone was watching the house, Jane had a hard time falling asleep that night. At one point she got up and, without turning on the lights, peered out the windows. The neighborhood was dark and silent.

The next morning Avery called Nancy and explained Danny's hearing was scheduled for early that afternoon. Over the receiver Jane overheard him say, "Once the judge determines the bail, I'll have him out in a matter of hours."

Nancy jotted down the time and courtroom location of the hearing. She then explained Jane's plans to leave immediately. "Can you pass that on to Danny?"

Avery agreed.

Since it would be a few hours, Jane climbed into Danny's Chevy Malibu and backed down the driveway. To ensure that nobody was following, she got on the freeway and opened the car up, the speedometer pushing past one hundred twenty miles per hour. Then she got on the frontage road and double-backed the way she came. She found Avery's office in downtown Sarasota.

Jane could see Avery's law office was also a cliché with its antique, dark wood furniture and leather-bound law books arranged on shelves. She noted a vintage safe in the corner and a wet bar complete with a bottle of Pappy Van Winkle's Family Reserve Bourbon. On the label was the namesake Pappy himself, an old man with a cigar in his mouth.

Avery sat in a leather-upholstered chair across from his polished mahogany desk and explained that he had spoken to Danny and relayed her request. Then he handed over a North Carolina driver's license of a woman a few years older, Lynette Foster, a curly haired brunette. There was no resemblance in the photograph. The mousy looking woman wore thick glasses and Jane said to him, "This won't work. She looks nothing like me."

"It's going to have to work, for now," Avery said.

"Who is she?"

"Victim of aggressive breast cancer, I'm afraid. But the driver's license is not critical as long as you don't get pulled over or take a flight." Avery handed over a MasterCard. "It's this credit card that you'll need more than anything else. Be conservative with it." He gave her his business card with a PIN number scribbled on the back. "You can draw cash at any ATM using this number, and the credit card bills will come to this office. I'll pay them from Danny's trust."

"Was this hard to get? I mean...a false identity like this?" she asked.

"Everything is available at a price, my dear. But

if you get arrested, just remember, you didn't get this from me. If they ask, you found a wallet."

"Thank you," she said.

Avery sat back and said, "You should know Danny was resistant at first and would rather have you all together. But I looked into your adversary, this Veronica Tattinger character, and what little I found...let's just say I convinced Danny that your plan to lay low is undoubtedly best."

Jane had no intention of telling him that laying low was not her plan at all. She'd continue to chase Veronica, no matter what, and finish the job she'd started. She asked, "What have you heard about her?"

"That she's ruined many lives."

"Who said so?"

"I have sources on both sides of the law," he said. Then he handed her a cell phone still in its plastic case. She could see it was nothing fancy, a model you'd see in a supermarket. "Stay in touch with this phone, registered as Lynn Foster, your new alias, and stop using yours."

At that moment it dawned on her. "That's how Veronica has been able to track me. Through my cell phone."

"Quite possibly. Turn off your old phone and remove the battery for now," he advised. "And please use this one until further notice." He stood and said, "Now if you'll excuse me, I've got to prepare for Danny's hearing."

Jane got up and said, "Thank you. I'll see you there."

"I suggest you do not attend the hearing."

"Why?"

"Just in case."

"Just in case of what?" she asked.

"Worst case scenario."

Back at home her mother helped Jane pack her suitcase. In addition to toiletries she added a photo of them smiling together taken at Jane's high school graduation.

"What are you doing?" Jane asked her mother. "You should keep this."

"So I'll always be with you," Nancy said, burying the frame under a sweater. Her mom then pulled a Colt .380 Mustang from under the bed and packed that too.

"Mom?" Jane said.

"Just in case," Nancy said. She added a second clip loaded with copper-headed bullets.

From her old cell phone Jane jotted down the numbers she'd need, Cooper's included. Jane gave her mother her new phone number and they made plans to meet in Sonoma. They hugged, pledged their love for each other in a tearful goodbye.

First she drove to Danny's garage. She used the hide-a-key to get in, went to the kitchen, and pushed the old refrigerator away from the wall for the outlet. She put her old cell phone's ringer on mute, plugged in the charger, and wedged the phone into the coils in the back of the appliance. She figured this was a place nobody would ever look. If Veronica was indeed tracking Jane's location through her cell phone, keeping the phone powered would make it appear as if Jane was still in Florida. Avery suggested she turn the phone off, but Cooper had said something outside the Starbucks that stuck in her mind, about the writings of Sun Tzu from the *Art of War*, something about, "When we are near, we must make the enemy believe we are far away." She leaned into the fridge and pushed it back.

On the same stretch of highway, Jane repeated the Chevy's blistering speed before she double-backed, the procedure to make sure she wasn't being tailed.

Lastly, she saw the nursing home and pulled off the highway. She drove through the concrete parking structure and found a non-descript Honda Accord that looked like it hadn't been driven in a while. She parked alongside the vehicle and swapped out the Florida license plates. The Honda got the Chevy's, and vice versa. It was a gamble the owner of the Honda wouldn't notice but a risk she felt she had to take. Now the Chevy could not be traced back to Danny.

An hour out of Sarasota, at a payphone in a nearly vacant Denny's, she called Cooper. His voicemail picked up so she left a message, "It's me, call me at this number." She had just finished the wedge of pickle and was about to take bite out of her club sandwich when the phone rang. She got up from the counter and picked up the receiver.

"Where are you?" she asked.

Cooper said, "Not far from Vandenberg Air Force Base in California. Where are you?"

"Listen to me. This is the deal, take it or leave it. We work as a team finding Veronica, but we don't kill her," Jane said. "Is that understood? We hand her over to the cops."

"Okay," he said.

"Say we won't kill her," she persisted.

"We won't kill Veronica."

"You have to promise me."

"I promise."

"I don't believe you."

"Eating jailhouse slop will be hell for Veronica, I assure you."

"What do you mean?" Jane asked.

"Over the years with her high-priced lawyers she's managed to slip out of every noose, but not this time. I have a plan that's going to put her away for a very, very long time."

"We're not together anymore," Jane said, "No intimacy whatsoever, or I won't help."

"I understand," he said.

"Because of you I'm running for my life," she said.

"I had no choice."

"I don't believe you."

"You have every right to hate me," he said, "and after we snag Veronica you'll never see me again. I agree, we work only as partners, but we don't have much time."

"How do you plan on catching her?" she asked.

"It's complicated. I'll explain everything. Where are you?"

"On my way."

CHAPTER 6

Jane carried the camera bag, Cooper the tripod. She'd brought along a portable umbrella but left her gun in the car. They walked the campus of California Polytechnic State University nestled in the rolling hills of San Luis Obispo. There was a heavy fog and the concrete pathways were damp.

Jane couldn't help but notice the students going about their day and wished she could turn back the clock. It wasn't that long ago that she was in school. Other than keeping up with her busy social calendar and getting to class on time, she hadn't a worry in the world. As she walked among the students Jane felt old even though the age difference was only a few years. She figured what separated her from these students was that she had real world problems, with life or death consequences. Her carefree days were gone forever.

Fueled by coffee and Red Bull, she'd driven straight through from Florida and only stopped for gas, food, and occasional shut eye. With the Colt .380 Mustang in her hand, she'd taken brief naps in the backseat of the Chevy parked at twenty-four-hour diners, curled up under a polyester throw blanket she bought at a roadside truck stop.

She'd arrived in Pismo Beach the day before, exhausted, and checked into a kitschy Polynesian-themed motel along the cliffs. She parked in an adjacent motel's lot just in case. The room overlooked the ocean across an uncrowded beach. Jane rewarded herself with a take-out pizza, took a long shower, then slept like a baby as the sound of the waves crashed beyond her balcony.

This morning she grabbed a cup of coffee in the lobby before she tended to her injured leg. She could see the wound was healing. Although annoying to deal with, at least the pain was gone. She thought the wound looked like a Frankenstein scar and it would be a long time before she could wear a dress. This was a battle scar for life, thanks to Veronica.

With the .380 Mustang in her purse, she headed out to meet Cooper. She was not entirely comfortable with him knowing where she was staying so she walked the shoreline and met him at entrance to the Pismo Beach Pier. He was there waiting and Jane reminded him theirs was strictly a working relationship.

Cooper nodded and said, "Fine. Understand the reason I need you is I can't do this myself. This gold is Veronica's escape hatch, and she desperately needs it." Then they set out for the campus in his nondescript rental car.

Jane and Cooper entered the university campus and followed the engraved signs before they found the history department. Professor Ricardo Gomez rose from behind his cluttered desk to greet them. "So nice to meet you," he said, extending his hand. The energetic, middle-aged professor sported a grey beard and wore round, John Lennon-style glasses.

"So kind of you to find the time on such short notice," Cooper said.

"I'm honored to be included in your project," Gomez said.

Cooper introduced Jane as his cinematographer. Having acted in low-budget movies, Jane was familiar with what the camera department did but never thought she'd masquerade as one of them. Jane considered the black and white photographs in the office, miners panning for gold in old-time San Francisco. There was a California history book on the professor's desk, his name as the author. This made sense since Cooper explained Gomez's expertise was the California Gold Rush.

"I've set aside a classroom," Gomez said. "Right this way." He grabbed his laptop and led them down the hallway asking, "So...why such interest in the *SS Yankee Blade*?"

"As I explained," Cooper said, "there's new-found evidence that there might have been more gold on that ship than the ship's manifest claims."

"A likely scenario," Gomez said. "The California Gold Rush drew its share of ruffians. The railroads and steamship companies were known to create two manifests, especially when shipping gold."

"To throw them off?" Cooper asked.

"That's right, and since Captain Randall abandoned her..." he said shaking his head. "It doesn't make sense. A captain is supposed to be the last one off a ship, but that was not the case on the *Yankee Blade.*"

The classroom had large windows that offered plenty of light. Jane suggested the professor sit in a chair with the classroom's white board partly in frame behind him. Cooper agreed and pulled up a chair beside the camera. Within a few minutes they were set up, a lavalier microphone on the lapel of the professor's jacket. Jane framed up the shot, confirmed it with Cooper, and they were ready to go.

"Rolling," she said, mimicking the lingo of an actual cinematographer.

After Cooper asked the professor to introduce himself, he asked, "What can you tell us about the *Yankee Blade*?"

"Most people think of steamships as Mark Twain-style paddleboats with tall smokestacks, like that one they have at Disneyland. But seafaring steamships of the time were much larger than riverboats, designed for speed, powered by side-wheels combined with sailing masts. The *Yankee Blade* was a state-of-the-art vessel when she was built in New York. Cornelius Vanderbilt, founder of the

New York Central Railroad, purchased the boat. Vanderbilt knew a thing or two about steam-powered transportation. He'd built a monopoly in railroads and shipping, and he sent the *Yankee Blade* to transport gold, passengers, and cargo between San Francisco and Panama during the height of the Gold Rush."

Jane could see Gomez had prepared for the interview and admired him for it. As a performer, she knew preparation was key.

Gomez went on to explain that in the mid-19th century there were only three routes to travel between the east and west coast, "Train, but that was time-consuming with many stops and a risk of robbers poaching the cargo. The second was sailing around the tip of South America which took longer and could be treacherous considering the currents. The preferable route was steaming to Panama then transporting passengers and cargo by small boats and mule train through the mosquito-ridden Isthmus of Panama, then sailing north again on another ship. Mind you this was a good fifty years before the Panama Canal was built. The *Yankee Blade* served the Pacific Ocean leg of this journey."

"Fascinating," Cooper said to encourage him. "Tell us about the shipwreck."

"There were eight hundred and twelve passengers and a hundred and twenty-two crew aboard the *Yankee Blade*. She was traveling southward too fast considering the fog. There's speculation," the professor said, leaning forward for emphasis, "that a bet was made."

"What kind of bet?" asked Cooper.

"Also leaving San Francisco for Panama at the time was the steamship *Sonora*, and the captains may have engaged in an unofficial race to Panama, with five thousand dollars on the line, according to the newspaper *Daily Alta California*. Once both ships left San Francisco Bay, the *Sonora* took the longer, safer route further out to sea, whereas Captain Randall hugged the coast, waters considerably more dangerous."

"Five thousand dollars was a lot of money back then," Cooper said.

"It's a lot of money now, just imagine it back then," Gomez said. He continued, "The fog grew thick"—motioning to the windows—"much like today, with visibility extremely low, and the *Yankee Blade* struck a pinnacle of rock off Point Arguello. It tore a gash in the ship's hull and she was wedged at an angle on the rocks." Gomez demonstrated with his hand.

Cooper had told Jane some of these details, but Gomez made the story so much more interesting. This professor was a bona fide storyteller.

Gomez went on, "It was obvious to those on board it was only a matter of time before the pounding surf would push the listed ship off the rocks to a watery doom. But for some unexplained reason, Captain Randall took command of the lifeboats instead, leaving his unqualified teenage son in charge of the ship."

"His teenage son?" Cooper asked.

"Yes. A captain leaving a sinking ship doesn't make sense, but to make matters even worse for those on board..." The professor paused for dramatic effect. "California had attracted a large number of lawless men unable to find fortune mining for gold. Bear in mind the state was just four years old and lawmen were few and far between. Bad guys on board took advantage of the situation and began to rob and murder passengers. Mind you, some of the passengers had struck gold in the fields and were heading back to the east coast with their hard-earned treasure, probably carried in money belts. Captain Randall would later claim to have been seeking safety for the women and children, but conflicting claims confuse whether he ever returned to the shipwreck and instead spent the night onshore while most of the passengers were on board fending for their lives. In the disorganized rescue effort a few of the lifeboats full of women and children sank, apparently loaded with too much weight. Drowned bodies of mothers clutching their children washed ashore."

Images of drowned children came to Jane and she felt a sudden pang of sadness. *How tragic.*

"Could these lifeboats been loaded with gold?" Cooper asked.

"Presumably."

Cooper shot a knowing look to Jane before he said, "I understand the San Francisco Mint was brand new at the time so, according to the manifest, there were gold coins aboard."

"That we know for sure. Back in the seventies divers salvaged some of these coins from the shipwreck, high-grade 1854 double eagle twenty-dollar pieces. Today, a standard twenty-dollar double eagle piece is worth over twelve hundred dollars, but the same coin traced to the *Yankee Blade* is worth well over ten thousand dollars at auction. Collectors authenticate the shipwreck coins from both a subtle die crack imperfection traceable to the first stamps of the San Francisco Mint, combined with the damage of sand and sea water over the years."

"So what happened next?" Cooper asked.

"With the stern of the ship underwater, throughout the night the *Yankee Blade* slipped lower and lower which forced the passengers to the aft of the already crowded boat. Fortunately the next morning the steamship *Goliath* came to her rescue, and the *Goliath*'s skipper, Captain Haley, risked his own ship drawing close enough to transport the surviving passengers to safety. Because of the limited capacity of the *Goliath* some of the passengers were left behind. They camped onshore and local ranchers supplied them with food and supplies until they were eventually rescued."

"And Captain Randall?"

"Captain Randall stood trial for his role in the disaster in a kangaroo court almost a year after its occurrence. A panel of his peers acquitted him of all charges."

"Acquitted him?"

"Yes."

"So he got away with it?"

"So much so that years later the *Santa Barbara Gazette* reported that a Captain Randall, commanding a small schooner, had succeeded in recovering gold from the wreck; his share penciled out to over eighty thousand dollars at the time."

"He got to keep the gold?" Cooper said.

"Yes. That's maritime law regarding shipwrecks: finders keepers. Randall retired but not before he returned to the site a few more times. He even helped chart maps of the area, his career apparently unblemished by the incident."

"What a rat," Cooper said.

"Indeed."

Indeed, Jane thought. *Who uses that word*? Professors, she guessed.

Gomez continued, "Thirty souls perished, some of them having jumped ship or were murdered by the ruffians. Call it cowardice, greed, or a combination of both, but Randall's negligence is what makes the wreck of the *Yankee Blade* such a tragic event."

"What's your opinion?" Cooper asked. "Is there gold still out there?"

"I wouldn't be surprised. Reportedly the ship's vault was underwater only minutes after she struck the rocks. Although pieces of the ship have been salvaged over the years, including a brass canon, the vault has never been found. And since 9/11 salvage efforts are impossible."

"Why's that?"

"The wreckage is off Vandenberg Air Force Base and security strictly prohibits access to the area."

They wrapped up the interview and Cooper thanked the professor. As Jane put the camera away, Gomez opened his laptop and he and Cooper explored Google Maps. From the satellite image bird's-eye view, Gomez pointed out where he approximated the ship sank, rocky clusters near small islands he said was the Vandenberg Marine Reserve. The satellite imagery depicted brown topsoil contrasting the shoreline of blue ocean. There were curvy lagoons and cliffs with the whitewash of crashing waves, evidence that there were many rocks just under the water's surface. Jane pointed out a cluster of white buildings and asked, "What's that?"

Gomez zoomed in for more detail, "Vandenberg Space Launch Complex 8."

She looked to Cooper. *You've got to be kidding.*

He gave her a subtle nod and Cooper thanked the professor again.

* * *

On the drive to Morro Bay Cooper explained that the long lost, hand-drawn map Veronica has in her possession does not necessarily detail where the ship sank but rather the caves onshore where, supposedly, Captain Randall hid the gold. Apparently the ship's purser drafted the map. But then he disagreed with how Randall handled the tragedy and kept it from him when Captain Randall returned to the scene. By then violent storms had altered the coastal geography and covered up the shoreline caves. "When Captain Randall returned," Cooper said, "he only salvaged a portion of the hidden gold. Gomez is right, he returned a few more times over the years but wasn't successful until finally he gave up. Treasure seekers have long searched for the ship's vault, but according to the purser's map, the one Veronica has, the vault was emptied before the ship went down."

"So the gold is in these caves?"

He nodded, "That's right."

"After all of these years?"

"Everyone has always focused on the shipwreck, not where the gold was stashed."

"How is Veronica going to find these caves?"

"Aided by sophisticated geological equipment used in the oil shale industry. It may take a while, a few weeks."

"A few weeks?"

"Unless they get lucky. Veronica is convinced she knows where to dig."

"All under the cloak of scientific study?" Jane said.

"That's the plan."

"And what if the Air Force finds out?"

"She plans on deceiving them but I have a plan."

CHAPTER 7

When they arrived in Morro Bay Jane was struck by the massive rock that overshadowed the bay. It looked like a giant molar tooth that stuck up at the edge of the shoreline, black, and seemed so out of place. She didn't realize how large it was until they drew closer.

Cooper parked the rental car on Embarcadero Street. Through binoculars they spied men on a yacht. "The trawler arrived from San Diego last week," Cooper explained, "and as you can see they're preparing it now. Once Air Force Space Command grants permission, they'll set out and anchor just off Vandenberg. They're supposed to be graduate students studying sea life but in reality they're nothing but scavengers."

Jane watched as one of them behind a welder's mask worked on the arm of a crane at the bow of the ship—the hot glow of the torch visible from a distance.

Cooper added, "Veronica will be on that boat."

She turned to him and asked, "When?"

"Could be any day now, could be next month. What I need you to do is a little reconnaissance."

"How so?"

Cooper produced a photo of a short-haired, tattooed guy that appeared to be in his early thirties. "By befriending Brendan Cassidy, the boat's captain."

"Me?"

"That's right."

"Why me?"

"Because he knows me. When Veronica and I were together I found Brendan for this job. He owns that yacht and has a lot of diving and salvage experience. You're going to be the girl he meets in the bar."

"What bar?"

Cooper thumbed over his shoulder. "A craft brew place he hangs out in just around the corner."

Jane craned her neck to look for the establishment he was talking about, "So I'm just going to walk up to him and say, 'Hey, sailor, when ya shoving off?'"

"You're an actress. Improvise."

"How do I do that?"

"Get him to open up. You'll find a way. I've seen you in action," he said, respect in his eyes. "You're a natural."

Jane felt a mix of both anger and sorrow. She had loved Cooper once. What was he suggesting? "You don't expect me to sleep with him, do you?"

"I'm not saying that."

"It sounds like you are."

"Just befriend the guy. Distract him enough so I

can get on that boat for five minutes. That's all I ask."

"But you're implying—"

"I'm not implying anything," he said, cutting her off. "He's not going to tell you what he's doing here, but he may clue you in to when they're heading out. We need to know that."

Jane returned to the binoculars just as the welder pulled up his mask. It appeared to be the same guy from the photo Cooper had shown.

"Is that him?" she asked.

"That's Brendan."

He was lean and sported a close-shaven beard, a ruggedly handsome surfer type. "What's he like?" she asked.

Cooper cleared his throat. "A crazy party boy with larceny in his soul."

"How so?"

"His father was a safe cracker and jewel thief, currently serving a stint in Rahway."

"Rahway?"

"It's a prison in New Jersey. As a young man Brendan wanted nothing to do with his father and joined the Navy to get away from the life. He excelled, became a SEAL, saw action in the Middle East, did a few tours, and then after an honorable discharge he started buying and selling boats. But he's had a hard time adjusting to civilian life. If there's ever a poster boy for post-traumatic stress disorder, you're looking at it. He's unpredictable and lives on the edge, his lifestyle far more extravagant than what a common boatyard broker can afford. His racket is insurance fraud, but on a Lloyds of London scale."

"How does that work?" she asked, watching as Brendan and one of the men moved an acetylene tank.

"He finds yacht owners who need to get out from under their...investments."

"Out from under?"

"The accessories and electronics, everything on a yacht, all are extremely expensive. He orchestrates it all so the boat owner purchases all sorts of upgrades that never make it on the vessel. He returns or resells them, then waits for the perfect storm and sets the stage for a disaster at sea. They sink the yacht and split the insurance money."

"So he's a pirate, like Veronica," Jane said.

"Precisely. He's got a clean record except for a few instances of physical abuse."

"What kind of abuse?"

"He's been known to slap around a girlfriend or two, that sort of thing. More than one has pressed charges. He has anger issues."

"So he's a bastard."

"Yes, he's a bastard," Cooper said. "And these men he's brought on, they're not boy scouts either, most of them ex-soldiers gone bad, or mercenary washouts."

She set the binoculars on the console, turned to

him and said, "And much like you, a life of crime is in his family."

"That's right."

Jane didn't know how to phrase it so just dived in. "How about you? You ever try to get away from the family business?"

"So you know about that?"

"I understand your father ran boiler rooms in Canada, sweepstakes scams that preyed on the elderly."

"Among other things," he said.

"Did you ever try to do something else?"

He shrugged, took a moment to think about it, then said, "I went to college. Concordia in Montreal. Studied economics."

"And?"

"Do you remember the old-school ventriloquist Shari Lewis? She had a white sock puppet named Lamb Chops, back in the fifties and sixties, *The Ed Sullivan Show* era."

Being an amateur magician Jane was familiar with Shari Lewis and her signature puppet. "Sure," she said.

"She was the only female ventriloquist in her day," Cooper said. "Well...I saw an interview with her and she told a story. She was just barely out of school when she found success on television, and eventually NBC gave Shari her own show. It replaced *Howdy Doody*."

Cooper telling *her* a show business story? That's

a first. Jane said, "*Howdy Doody* creeped me out. All marionettes are freaky."

"I agree. Sock puppets are better. The way Shari tells it one day she met Queen Elizabeth, who apparently really liked her act. The Queen asked, 'How does a young girl become a ventriloquist?' Shari explained that she grew up in New York and that her father was a magician. Mayor LaGuardia named him New York City's official magician, and Shari had learned the basics of ventriloquism from him."

"Okay..." Jane said, wondering where this was leading.

"So, the Queen considered this and said, 'Dear, I suppose we *all* tend to do what our parents do, don't we?'"

Jane laughed. "Okay, but Queen Elizabeth doesn't have a choice. She's born into it."

"I was born into it too," Cooper said.

Jane thought about her mother, wondered how she was doing, and then trained the binoculars back on the yacht.

"After we confirm Veronica's on that boat," Cooper continued, "and it's anchored outside Vandenberg, we blow the whistle, claiming they're preparing for an act of terrorism."

"Terrorism?"

"Because of something special I'll plant, everyone on that boat will go away for a very, very long time."

"What will you plant?" she asked.

"I'll show you," Cooper said and opened the car door. Jane emerged from the passenger side while keeping an eye on the yacht. Cooper opened the trunk of the car to reveal a black plastic Pelican case.

"What's that?"

He snapped the handles and opened the large case to reveal the military-grade weapon and said, "It's a FIM-92 Stinger."

Jane was shocked at the sight of the single-shot bazooka fit snuggly into the foam of the case. "Holy shit," she said.

Cooper explained, "A shoulder-fired, surface-to-air missile launcher. When the crew is off that boat, and you've distracted Brendan, I'll sneak this aboard and hide it in the engine room."

"So that's the plan? Get the surfer off his boat?"

"He won't leave his yacht unless one of the crew is on board. The rest of the guys don't sleep on the yacht, so..."

"I don't get it."

"You'll make his acquaintance then distract him enough so he'll be forced to leave the yacht. That's when I'll move in. Then, once Veronica gets on and they're sitting outside Vandenberg we tip off the feds."

Realizing the weapon had to be extremely illegal Jane asked, "Where'd you get it?"

"Everything's available for a price, and this

didn't come cheap, believe me. I had it smuggled from Chechnya by way of Montreal," he said. "It's questionable if it actually works, but that doesn't matter because it doesn't have to. The government just has to find it in their possession."

"So that's the plan, frame Veronica?" she asked.

"For starters. Then we let nature take its course."

It seemed so elaborate and she asked, "Why not just grab her before she gets on the boat then hand her over to the cops?"

"Because for the first time in her life she won't be able to snake out of it."

"How can you be sure?"

"Bail is rejected in cases of domestic terrorism," Cooper said. He slammed the trunk and added, "She'll be fucked."

CHAPTER 8

Jane smiled at Brendan.

He smiled back.

Moments ago she and Cooper were watching as Brendan left his yacht. She went to the bar and then, as if on cue, Brendan entered the Libertine Pub, found a stool, and ordered an IPA. The bartender, a woman with tattooed arms, poured his draft and they chatted for a moment. Jane could see they knew each other. The smell of fried fish wafted from the kitchen.

Cooper had explained this was Brendan's daily routine, a couple of hours off the boat for dinner and a few beers before he'd return to the yacht and relieve the last of the crew.

Before he got there she'd ordered a Sprite and lime in a highball glass to make it look like she was sipping a gin and tonic. Even though she had the .380 Mustang in her purse, Jane was nervous.

One exchange of smiles became two. It wasn't long before Brendan moved over, introduced himself as "Brad," and took the stool next to her.

Jane played along. "I'm Sarah. Where are you from?"

"The Bay area."

"I moved here from L.A.," she said, weaving a little bit of truth into her narrative. She'd already invented her backstory. She was a traveling nurse recently hired at the local hospital.

When she asked what he did, Brendan boasted, "I'm a skipper."

"A what?"

"Owner/operator of a commercial vessel. You can see it from here," he said and got up from his stool. "I'll show ya."

"Luxury sailboat?" she asked, following him to the window.

"Not a sailboat, but it's got its comforts."

She thought of her purse and the gun back on the bar. She considered turning back to get it but thought it might look suspicious, like she was hiding something. "It's a research vessel," he explained, pointing it out. Jane could see two of the crew working on deck as Brendan went on, "We're a scientific team studying ocean mammals for the Marine Life Protection Act."

"That's cool," Jane said. "What kind of mammals?"

"Whales and dolphins mostly," he said.

"Awesome," she said with a smile, knowing it was all a lie, his fictional cover story. Since Veronica had named her pleasure yacht the *Anne Bonny*, Jane asked him, "What's the name of your boat?"

"*Maenads.*"

Jane raised an eyebrow.

"In Greek mythology maenads are female worshippers of Dionysus, the god of wine."

"Worshippers?"

"Think of it as his lady posse. Through the ages Maenads are depicted as scantily clad maidens."

"God of wine, huh? Sounds like they're party girls," Jane said.

"Got that right. My vessel was named by the previous owner. Since it's bad luck to change the name of a boat, I kept it."

"So you're the captain of a boat named after a half-naked party girls," Jane teased.

"I didn't name her."

They returned to the bar and he offered to buy her a drink. Jane agreed on a Chardonnay but wished she had eaten more of a lunch. He elaborated on what it was like captaining a boat and added that he had served as a Navy SEAL. Jane could see he was trying to impress her. By the way Brendan looked at her it was clear sex was on his mind. Although men in flannel weren't necessarily her type, she found him attractive, and charming. She'd never think of flirting with a guy like this had she not been undercover. The fact that he'd been physically abusive to girlfriends came to mind.

She could see Brendan was fishing to find common interest. When a guy wearing a leather jacket and sporting wide mutton chop sideburns strolled past reeking of marijuana, the subject of legalization came up. It wasn't long before he asked if she wanted to duck out to sample a bit of, "Da kine indica," as he phrased it.

Jane explained, "I wish I could but I work in a hospital, so...drug tests."

"Seriously?"

"Random, supposedly, but I've never been asked to take one. It's because we work around pain killers."

"Oh, I see, like some nurse sneaking a patient a placebo while keeping one or two for herself?" he said.

"I'm sure it happens," Jane said.

"OxyContin? Morphine? Tylenol with codeine?"

"I administer all that stuff."

Brendan then said, "Can I ask you something? And please don't take this the wrong way."

"Sure."

"Got a boyfriend?"

"It's complicated," she said and found herself blushing. She tore the fringe of her cocktail napkin out of nervousness. It was clear he had sex on his mind.

"That a yes or no answer?" he playfully inquired.

Jane knew she had to keep his prospects alive in order to distract him and said, "I'm not seeing anyone. I was, but...he betrayed me."

"Cheated?"

Jane thought of Veronica and Cooper together

before she said, "So to speak. But he was with this other woman before me. Then when he went back to her she betrayed him, so...c'est la vie."

"No way."

"Yes way."

"As beautiful as you are...he was a fool," he said.

"She was very persuasive, this other woman, and far more beautiful than me."

At that moment her phone buzzed with text from Cooper, "*How's it going?*" Jane replied with a thumbs up emoticon. "A nurse friend," she said for his benefit. After she felt she'd made enough of a memorable impression, Jane excused herself by claiming she had to meet her.

"Ask your friend to meet us here," he proposed.

"She's making dinner at her apartment."

"Okay then. What's your number?" he asked. "We can meet for lunch. I'm not going to be in Morro Bay long, but if you can find the time...?"

"Sure," she said before realizing she hadn't memorized the new phone number on the throw-away phone Avery Weeks had given her. "Better yet," she said, "let me text you. What's yours?" she asked.

Brendan offered his number as she pecked it into her phone. Then she texted out the name she'd given him, "Sarah," and pressed send. Seconds later his phone chirped and he said, "Cool. Got it."

"Really nice meeting you," she said getting up and grabbing her purse.

"Seriously, let's grab lunch or another drink sometime," he said and nudged her arm. "Whenever it works for you and your schedule. It would be great to see ya again."

"I'd like that. Thanks for the drink," she said.

"Cheers."

Jane could feel his eyes on her back as she walked out the door.

On the drive back to Pismo Beach, Jane filled Cooper in. The wine she had with Brendan put her in a good mood. "I'm certain I made an impression," she said.

"You always make an impression."

"What does that mean?"

"You have charisma. I saw it when we met in Jeremy's acting class."

"Charisma?"

"A spark."

On the one hand Jane liked the compliment, but on the other she didn't want to encourage him. She changed the subject and asked, "So tell me again, how do we plan to get this rocket launcher on Brendan's boat."

"After the crew leaves for the day, and he's alone, you're going to feign distress. Car trouble."

"Aren't you afraid," Jane asked, "that we'll get pulled over and the cops discover that thing in your trunk?"

"They'd have to be tipped off, and nobody knows I have it, except you."

"When do we plant it on the boat?"

"As soon as possible."

"And where do you think Veronica is now?"

"No telling. She can't be far. She'd feel compelled to supervise the expedition."

"And after the feds arrest her, what will happen to Billy?"

"I'll take him home to Canada. The story I told you about Shari Lewis, the ventriloquist...I'm determined to break that chain. Setting him on a straight path is my stab at redemption."

"Having a midlife conscience, are you?"

"My brother is dead, my father has advanced dementia. Billy is the only family I've got left. I'd be happy to just live a quiet, suburban life."

Jane asked, "Is Billy going to play hockey?"

"Damn straight."

"You'll teach him?"

"He's my son."

"You'd have to kidnap him, though, right?"

"What do you mean?"

"The cops will want answers and you're supposed to be dead."

"Veronica lives off the grid, and so does Billy. He's not a U.S. citizen because he was born in the Turks and Caicos. Nobody will lay claim to him, except me."

They drove the rest of the way in silence.

To put herself at ease, Jane still felt it best Cooper not know which one of the many motels she was staying at so she had Cooper drop her off at the Pismo Beach Pier. They made plans to meet back there the next morning.

She walked up Pomeroy Avenue and ordered a takeout sandwich at Mo's Smokehouse BBQ. Then she walked around downtown Pismo Beach to make sure she wasn't being followed. She slipped into a nail spa and cut out through the back door. When she was satisfied nobody could be tailing, Jane walked back to her motel room at the Kon Tiki Inn. She sat on her private balcony to eat her tri-tip sandwich as the sound of waves crashed in the distance. Then she called her mother.

"We're on the road, driving to California," Nancy said. "Avery took care of everything, like Danny said he would. Where are you?"

"Working at my friend's melodrama near Pismo Beach," Jane lied.

"Are you going to be in the show?"

"Just working the box office and serving concessions for now. I've got to pay my dues there. That's how it works. But everyone's been really nice."

"We'll come see you!"

"Wait until I'm in a show," Jane said.

"The racing team is just a few points shy to qualify for Nationals. Danny's certain we can get them in Sonoma."

Familiar with the region from its wine, Jane had never been to Sonoma County but knew it was north of San Francisco. She held images in her mind of mountainside vineyards, but not necessarily a dragstrip. She asked, "When do you get there?"

"We're driving straight through without stopping so probably tomorrow. Where's Pismo Beach?"

"South a few hours," Jane said.

"You have to come see Danny race."

"Okay," she said, even though she wasn't sure if it was possible.

"How ya doin', Jane?" she heard Danny pipe in.

"Let me put you on speaker," her mother said.

A second later Danny's voice became clear and he asked, "How was the drive?"

"The Chevy served me well. I made really good time. That thing's got guts."

"I knew she would. You doin' all right? Your mother misses you."

"I miss her too. Both you guys. How was jail?"

He teased, "You know as much as I what it's like to be in the pen."

"I bet Florida's jailhouse slop is better than what they serve in California."

"I highly doubt that. When we get together we'll compare notes."

Jane heard her mother's nervous laugh before she said, "That's all behind us now. We're family and nothing is going to keep us apart."

Jane hoped her mother was right and said, "Call me when you guys get settled."

"We will. Love you."

"Love you, too."

After she hung up Jane finished the sandwich and washed it down with the rest of the bottle of wine she'd bought the night before. She thought about what her mother had said, *we're family*, and then Cooper's plans to rescue his son. *What's more important than family?*

Out of curiosity, Jane searched on her phone and pulled up a satellite geography map of Vandenberg Air Force Base, similar to what the professor had done on his laptop. It featured an overlay grid which displayed the base perimeter. On another site a map denoted both active and abandoned missile sites along the thirty-five square miles of restricted coast. From the photos she could see many of the silos were decaying remnants from the Cold War.

She learned that the tracks of Amtrak's Pacific Surfliner cut through the base and hugged the scenic coast.

This all seemed so crazy, long lost gold on restricted government land, buried for over one hundred and fifty years. After searching legitimate sites, Jane came across the conspiracy theory ones that claimed there was a labyrinth of underground tunnels connecting Vandenberg's launch pads, all remnants of decaying infrastructure from the Cold War.

Exhausted from the long day, she put her phone on the charger on the bedside table then pulled down the Tahitian floral bedspread and crawled into bed.

CHAPTER 9

It was late afternoon when Jane and Cooper sat in the rental car parked up the hill. As to not be noticed, they had moved around a few times. This position offered a good view of the yacht, but not too obvious. Earlier that same day Jane found a skin-colored bandage to cover the ugly scar on her leg. She purchased a snug, mini-cocktail dress, a pair of leather high-heels, and a matching purse big enough to fit the Colt. Again she'd call on her acting skills. This ensemble was the right wardrobe for a scene about seduction.

"It's freezing," Jane said to Cooper, fighting off a chill. "Can you turn on the heater?" A damp, cold mist hung in the air.

Peering through binoculars Cooper said, "Not a good idea. A running car might draw attention."

"Easy for you to say, you've got a jacket."

"You wear it," he said, and started to remove it.

"No," Jane said, angered. "Forget it."

"Why not?"

"Because I don't want it."

"If you're cold then—"

"I don't want your jacket," Jane snapped. The idea of wearing *his* jacket did not appeal to her.

"All right. Let me know if you change your mind." He considered the yacht again and said, "Looks like everyone else is gone," before he set the binoculars on the dash.

Jane caught him sneak a peek at the top of her thighs below the hemline before he said, "Let's see if you can coax Brendan off his boat."

"This dress is too short," Jane said, pulling it down.

"You picked it."

"You told me to get something sexy."

He looked at her and said, "You are."

"Stop it!"

Cooper raised his hands in surrender, "I know, strictly business, as you said. I'm just saying..."

"Why did I allow you to talk me into this?"

"Look, we're almost there. Get him off the boat, I'll plant the weapon, and then you're done. Once Veronica shows up..."

"I should have gotten a shawl, or something. And this hemline is too short."

"Just have confidence that you look great."

Jane felt a sense of déjà vu. It was as if she was back in L.A. where she and Cooper were attempting to hook Alexander Wolff into the diamond scheme. It brought back the memory of Cooper's betrayal. But now here he was again complimenting her on the way she looked, stirring up memories of their romance. She considered telling him to shut up but instead dug out her phone. "So how do I phrase it?"

"Keep the text simple. Say your car won't start. Give it a minute to see if he responds. Then call him."

"And if that doesn't work?" she asked.

"Then we'll find another way," Cooper said and started the car.

"Can you turn the heater on now?"

"Okay." He obliged, fumbled with the controls on the dash. They drove down the hill and parked on Embarcadero Street near a cluster of shops and restaurants. Cooper searched below until he found the latch and released the hood of the car. They both got out of the car, Jane finding her balance in her new high heels. Cooper popped the hood and, near the ignition wires, pulled out an electronic chip. He put it in his pocket, slammed the hood, and went around to the back of the car to open the trunk.

Jane followed, her heels wavering on the damp pavement.

Cooper struggled with the bulky black case, and Jane could see the weapon was heavy. He pulled it out, handed Jane the keys and said, "Give me a few minutes to get near the boat, then call."

"Okay."

He carried the black case toward the water.

As instructed, Jane sat behind the wheel and waited a few minutes before she texted Brendan,

"*Help. My car won't start.*" She waited but there was no response. After a few minutes she dialed. From this vantage point she could not see the boat.

"Hello?"

"Hey, it's me Sarah. From yesterday."

"Sarah the nurse?" She picked up on his enthusiasm.

"Yeah, that's right. Hey, sorry to bother you, but I'm on my way to a fundraising event and my car won't start. I was shopping for shoes over here, not far from your boat."

"Where?"

"I'm parked outside a bunch of shops. I've got nobody else to call. Can you lend me a hand?"

"Now?"

"Yeah."

"Where are you?"

"Like I said, not far from your boat."

They stayed on the phone until he found her. When Jane stepped out of the car his eyes lit up. She could see he didn't expect her to be dressed up. "Thank you so much, I'm going to be late for this thing and I don't know what happened," she said handing over the keys. After smiling at her for a second he climbed in the car and tried to start it. The starter turned over but the ignition did not fire. He got out and popped the hood.

"Weird that it won't start," Jane said.

"Where are you headed?" he asked.

"A cocktail reception near the hospital."

He looked over the engine and said, "The starter works so it's not the battery. These new cars..."

"Just my luck."

"I'd drive you but I don't have a car. I've got a moped on the boat."

"I'll just Uber it, I guess," she said and pulled out her phone, "Or maybe I just blow this whole thing off."

"Nobody's expecting you?" he asked.

"Donna, a nurse friend of mine, but I'm so new over there nobody will miss me." She let that hang for a moment then proposed. "I'll call a tow truck from the bar."

"A mighty fine idea," Brendan said, "but we'd need to go to a place where I can keep an eye on my boat," he said pointing to Dutchman's Seafood, a restaurant at the edge of the water.

"I could use a drink," Jane said. "Give me a second." She took her time going through the car to collect her things, figuring she needed to delay him as long as possible. "I'll call my friend and let her know not to expect me," Jane said. Brendan waited as she feigned a phone conversation with the fictitious co-worker Donna telling her she had "car trouble" and "may or may not make it." Then she texted Cooper to let him know Brendan was with her. She could see Brendan was getting impatient, and when she felt she couldn't delay anymore Jane grabbed her purse and joined him on the sidewalk.

Dutchman's Seafood was a nautical-themed, waterfront eatery with old-school brass fixtures and paintings of clipper ships on the walls. Brendan chose a bar table which afforded a view of his yacht. Jane gazed but could not see Cooper near the boat.

The cocktail waitress arrived and Brendan ordered a beer. Jane ordered wine and then, to buy time, fried calamari. After the waitress left she asked him, "When we met you asked me if I had a boyfriend,"—attempting to divert his attention from the yacht—"so, what about you? Seeing someone?"

He gave her a smile. "It's been a long time since I've had a girlfriend...or been with anyone for that matter."

She didn't believe him and teased with, "I doubt that. I'm willing to bet you have a girl in every port."

"Hardly."

"Yeah, right."

"Seriously. The sea is my mistress."

"Where'd you get that?" Jane questioned with playful cynicism, "From a Gordon Lightfoot song or something? 'Brandy?'"

"If you're talking about 'Brandy You're a Fine Girl,' Looking Glass recorded that tune," he said, "Lightfoot wrote 'The Wreck of the Edmund Fitzgerald.'"

"You know what I mean," she said, "sailors

breaking their girl's hearts because they're called to the sea."

"You've had yours broken, haven't you?"

She didn't expect that and said, rhetorically, "Haven't we all, at some point?" She glanced out to the yacht and was surprised to see Cooper on the docks. When Brendan followed her gaze Jane was quick to distract him, "You haven't answered my question. Are you seeing someone or not?"

"I'm not," he said.

Jane gave him a flirtatious smile and held her gaze for an extra moment before she looked away. It was the same non-verbal exchange she'd shared with Cooper on the first night they'd made love. She twirled her cocktail napkin as she felt his eyes upon her. She looked back to find his eyes were still locked and said, "What?"

"Nothing." He glanced to the bar for a moment, then returned his attention and said, "I'm no Casanova, that's for damn sure. Just an average guy out there saving seals."

"Navy SEALS?"

"No, the real thing now."

"I'm just teasing," she said.

"So tell me, who broke your heart?"

"Someone I used to work with," Jane confessed.

"A doctor?"

"No. A salesman," Jane said, considering the profession a realistic portrayal of Cooper—a con man and master of persuasion.

"He was a fool to let you go," he said.

"There was someone else."

"He made a mistake," he said, and sipped his beer before he proposed, "What do you say I show you my yacht?"

Here it goes Jane thought, *he's asking me back to his place.* She wondered what the captain's quarters on the yacht could possibly be like before she said, "We've got calamari coming."

"No rush," he said and looked out to the boat. Jane followed his gaze to make sure Cooper wasn't there. She could not see him.

"When are you setting out?" Jane asked.

"It depends on..." he started to say just as his cell phone rang. He reached into his pocket and pulled it out. He looked at the display, furrowed his brow, and said, "Sorry, I've got to take this." He got up and accepted the call with a formal, "This is Brendan."

Jane realized he'd made a critical mistake. He'd spoken his real name into the phone as opposed to alias the "Brad" he'd claimed to be when they first met. Brendan excused himself and searched for a quiet spot near the men's room to take the call.

She texted Cooper, "*Still with him.*"

After a moment she overheard Brendan say, "I've got it covered, Veronica. We're all set."

Veronica.

The realization hit her. He was talking with Veronica. Jane didn't know what to do. She got up to eavesdrop, approached the alcove to the restrooms and overheard him say, "Equipment is on board and my crew is standing by," before he turned and noticed her.

Jane gave him a forced smile and pointed to the door of the woman's room. He stepped aside and she brushed past him. Once inside, she stood at the door and trained her ear on the conversation. Jane caught a few snippets before Brendan asked, "A rocket launch? How long does that take? Okay, if we have to come back to Morro Bay and wait it out that's okay, I won't give up the boat slip."

Jane texted Cooper, "*He's on the phone with Veronica*!"

There was a moment of silence, and she wasn't sure if he'd walked away or not, but then she heard him ask, "So you're saying we shove off Friday? Got it. I'll check the weather again but it appears clear through the weekend."

Jane did the math in her head. Friday was a few days away. Then her phone buzzed. It was Cooper's text response "*Done. Get away from him.*"

She texted back "*Fix the car. I'll meet you there.*"

Jane knew she had what she needed, a clear idea when Veronica would board the yacht. And now that the missile launcher was stowed on his yacht her job was done. She breathed a sigh of relief, gave it a few minutes, washed her hands, and then returned to the table to find Brendan picking at the fried calamari with his fork. He gave her a smile as she sat down.

"Everything all right?" she said.

"Yeah. Just business."

"Who was it?" she asked to gauge his reaction.

"A marine scientist I'm working with."

Marine scientist? Jane thought, *total bullshit.* "So when do you all go to save the whales?" she asked.

"Not sure yet," he said before he motioned to her wine glass and said, "Want another?"

Jane pulled her purse close and said, "Can't, the tow truck is on its way."

"You called a tow truck?" he asked, surprised.

"That was the idea."

"What about touring my boat?"

"Some other time."

"Look, I'm sorry I had to take that call, but..."

"It's not that. I'm worried about my car. I've got to get to work tomorrow."

She could see he was mad so Jane feigned that she received a text, pulled her phone from her purse. "Oh, there they are now." She gave him a smile and said, "Thanks for the drink."

"What's the rush? Let's have dinner together."

"You're sweet, but I've got to work tomorrow," she said getting up. She could see he was disappointed and said, "Call me," to soften the blow.

"Wait up, I'll help you," he said reaching for his wallet.

"Thanks, Brendan," she said, using his real name. Jane saw the surprised reaction on his face. "That's you're real name, right?" she asked. "At least the one you used on the phone?"

He stammered, not knowing what to say, face turning red with anger. She'd caught him.

Jane spun on her heels and strolled out, feeling his eyes on her back. She figured it would take a minute or two for the waitress to bring Brendan the check and hoped it was enough time for Cooper to put the chip in the car—and make a fast getaway.

CHAPTER 10

Although she was exhausted, Jane tossed and turned in her sleep. Something didn't feel right, but she couldn't put her finger on it. Morning came and she pulled up Google Maps on her phone. Sonoma County was about a four-hour drive. Since she had a few days, Jane made the decision to visit her mother. She'd call Cooper from the road.

She checked out of the motel and hit the road. Outside Pismo Beach she found a stretch of two-lane highway and floored it for a half a mile. She cut onto a dirt road off the highway, shut off the engine, and gave it a good ten minutes. Then she double backed. Only after she was confident she wasn't being followed, Jane pulled over under the shade of an oak tree and checked the map again. She had the time so decided to take the scenic route, the Pacific Coast Highway heading north.

She called Cooper, "I'm getting out of town for a few days," she said, not wanting to offer too many details. "But I'll be back before Friday."

"Your job is done here," he said. "You really don't have to stick around. Go back to Florida. It's a waiting game until she gets on that boat."

Jane said, "I want to see her in handcuffs. But

more importantly, I want her to see me."

"Realize the arrest will happen on the base."

"There's got to be a perp walk, right? And they won't hold her on the Air Force Base, will they?"

"I don't know."

"I want Veronica to see me, even if it's in the courtroom for her preliminary hearing."

"Why's that important?"

"She tried to kill me."

"She tried to kill both of us."

"I need closure. What are you going to do?" she asked.

"I've checked into a motel in Morro Bay with a view of the yacht. Watching it now. When Veronica boards, and I know they're anchored off Vandenberg, I'll drop the dime."

"Call me if you see anything," she said. "I'm not going far."

"Where are you going?"

"I'd rather not say," she said.

"You still don't trust me?"

"What do you think?"

He said nothing.

"I'm a phone call away," Jane said.

"Fair enough."

Winding north on Highway 1, she was in awe of the rugged natural beauty of the coastal drive—dramatic cliffs and rocky beaches. Maneuvering the vintage muscle car through the curves made it even more exhilarating. She stopped a few times to get out and take in the majestic view. She'd seen photos in magazines but never realized how magnificent it was. At one scenic overlook there was a patch of fog off the coast and she imagined the fateful *Yankee Blade* hugging the shoreline as it steamed past so many years ago.

In Big Sur she considered checking into one of the tiny roadside motels but it was not something she wanted to do alone, and besides, she'd already told her mom she was on her way. *Someday,* she promised herself.

She stopped in Carmel for lunch. At a quaint bistro Jane sat outside under the shade of a cypress tree and ate what she considered the best turkey sandwich she'd ever had. The sliced turkey breast was cut off the bird, and the sandwich had a smoky chipotle dressing spread on its crispy baguette.

Afterward she took a stroll, truly enchanted by the sleepy coastal town. It felt like something out of a storybook. She found a wine shop and picked up a couple bottles of red that she guessed her mom would like.

Above Monterey she segued onto Highway 101, the scenic part of the drive behind her. When she reached Sonoma Raceway later that afternoon Jane drove past the grandstands and found the cluster of campers and trailers near the pit sheds at the end. She recognized Danny's trailer from a distance.

"Oh, Jane," her mother said, giving her a big hug. "I was so worried about you."

"What are you worried about?" Jane asked.

"A mother worries," she replied. "Always."

"I'm fine."

Danny came from the pit shed with a rag in his hand, his crew tinkering on the dragster behind him. "How's the old Chevy treating you?" he asked.

Jane turned to the Malibu and wished she'd taken it to the car wash before she'd arrived, out of respect since his pride and joy was on loan. "It's been running really well," she said and went on to explain how beautiful the drive up Pacific Coast Highway was. What she didn't mention was that she'd often used the muscle car's speed to ensure nobody was following. Sure, there was always the chance of getting pulled over and the cops not buying her fake ID, but she took that risk for peace of mind.

"I'll change her oil," Danny said, thumbing to the pit shed behind him. "She's got to be overdue."

Jane thought it interesting that he called the Chevy Malibu a *she*. Jane had never thought of vehicles, or boats for that matter, to be gender specific. She remembered that Veronica's boat was named *Anne Bonny*, and Brendan's yacht christened *Maenads*, both named after women. She wondered if maybe the fate of the *Yankee Blade*, or even the *Titanic* for that matter, would have been different had they been given feminine names.

"We're having burgers tonight," her mother

said, pointing to the grill and the prepared fixings.

"Sounds good," Jane said, even though she wasn't hungry.

While Danny went back to his work on the dragster, Jane opened one of the bottles of wine she'd brought and helped Nancy make dinner. She asked her mother why she'd set the gas grill so far away from the pit shed.

"In case of fuel spill," she explained.

Jane noted the no smoking signs all around them.

They cooked the burgers and set them on picnic tables nearby. The men arrived after washing up, most of them grabbing a can of beer as opposed the wine Jane had brought. She recognized most of the guys from the shop back in Florida. One of the younger ones, Luke, went out of his way to greet her and make small talk. He was nice, but she felt they had little in common. Her mother seemed to encourage Luke, and that embarrassed Jane. Aside, she accused, "Trying to get me married, Mom?"

"Grandchildren wouldn't be such a bad thing."

"I'm not ready for that."

"When the time is right, you'll know it," she said, then whispered, "But don't wait too long."

The thought of having a child and being responsible for another person's life while staying one step ahead of Veronica's vengeance brought a chill to Jane's spine. What if Cooper's plan failed? What would she do then? Where could she go where Veronica couldn't find her?

After dinner wrapped up, and as the sun was setting, the crew rolled the dragster into the trailer, locked it up, and they went back to the hotel. Just as he had before, Danny arranged an adjoining room in the hotel so Jane could be near them. She still had his Colt .380 Mustang in her purse and wondered what firearm Danny had brought along.

When her mother was in the shower, Jane asked Danny, "When you were on the run years ago, did you often feel like you were being watched?"

"What do you mean?"

"I feel like a dark shadow is hovering over me all the time. It's driving me crazy."

"I felt that way, too," he admitted, "for a long time."

"I don't know if it's real or my imagination." He said nothing and Jane pressed, "What do you think? Should I be worried?"

"Paranoia not such a bad thing if it keeps you alert."

"Why do you say that?"

"I don't want your mother to worry, so don't say anything to her."

She nodded.

In a lowered voice he said, "Back home...I noticed there were a few unannounced visitors, more than normal."

"Like who?"

"A UPS guy came to the garage and had me sign

for something that was just junk mail, nothing I'd ordered. I got the feeling he was checking my place out."

"Looking for me?"

"Or checking on me. Hard to say."

"What else?"

"There was a door-to-door salesman came by the house one night selling Kirby vacuums. Nobody does that anymore, do they? Door-to-door vacuum salesmen? Maybe I'm being paranoid too, but at the time my gut told me these guys weren't what they appeared to be."

"I've got a confession to make," Jane said. "I silenced my old cell phone, put it on its charger, and hid it behind the refrigerator in your garage."

Danny raised an eyebrow.

Jane continued, "In case Veronica was tracking me through that phone, which I suspect she was. I didn't want to turn it off so it would go completely dead. I wanted her to think I was still in Florida."

"Clever."

Jane considered telling him about Cooper's caper to trap Veronica at the base but felt it best to not divulge those details. She was afraid he'd insist she stay with them and she really wanted to see it through. Instead Jane asked, "How about your case? What does Avery Weeks say?"

"He claims the government doesn't have much of a case and they won't necessarily pursue it because it was such a long time ago. If it had been a mid-level drug dealer instead of an undercover agent who died in the line of duty they wouldn't have made a big deal out of it anyway."

"I'm sorry I brought this all down on you."

"Ah...I brought it upon myself," Danny said, "I didn't bank on my past catching up with me after all these years, but I suppose that's the one thing nobody can truly shed."

"What's that?"

"The sins of our past."

"But we can repent," Jane said, "Can't we?"

"That we can, darlin'. That we can."

CHAPTER 11

Jane awoke with a headache.

At first she attributed it to the red wine from the night before, then realized it was more than that—a sickness lingering, her body aching, possibly the beginnings of the flu. Nancy gave her a few Advil and made a cup of coffee from the single serve Keurig in the hotel room. While everyone else converged in the hotel's complimentary breakfast room, Jane took her time getting ready. She didn't have much of an appetite. She put her hair up and pulled on linen pants and a light cotton top. She put a few Advil in her pocket.

When they arrived at the racetrack and emerged from the air-conditioned comfort of Danny's truck, Jane could see it was going to be a hot day. The temperatures in Pismo Beach and along the Central Coast were mild with a gentle sea breeze. In comparison the inland air was dry and stagnant. The blazing sun made itself known early in the day.

"You'll need this," Nancy said as she handed Jane a credential badge. It was a laminated card to wear around her neck that read "Pit Crew." She then gave her a handful of foam ear plugs. "And you're going to need these, too."

"What are they?" said Jane.

"Ear protection."

Danny's crew pulled the dragster from the shade of the pit shed. They made last minute adjustments and everyone, including Jane and her mother, helped push the race car to the area behind the grandstands to queue it up for its first race. Other teams were doing the same, and Jane asked Danny, "Can't you just drive the car over?"

"She's not geared for that," he said.

There it was, *she* again. *So a dragster is a she, too?* Danny further enlightened her while pointing to the chrome engine block, "There's no radiator, and no starter on board either."

"Why not?"

"Extra weight we don't need. It's about speed and horsepower." Jane still did not understand. "Once she's warmed up," Danny continued, "we run her full bore for everything she's got. Then we get her back to the pit for some TLC."

"Tender loving care," her mother said in answer to Jane's quizzical look.

Jane knew that acronym and said, "Oh, right."

Danny continued, "Before she can even cool down we'll rebuild her for the next race. Pistons, rods, bearings, even the clutch; everything needs to be taken apart and put back together again."

"And all within seventy-five minutes," Nancy said. "These are the rules."

"I get it," Jane said, even though she didn't, but

she came to realize why Danny needed the crew. This was obviously a lot of work. She could see the sport attracts guys who like to take things apart and put them back together again.

"You'll see," her mother said.

A large crowd had already begun to arrive and fill up the grandstands. She'd been to outdoor concerts and occasional college football games, but never anything like this. RVs filled the parking lot. Entire families swarmed in, braving the heat. The fans were primarily male, but there was a percentage of women too, girlfriends and wives mostly, and grandmas tagging along.

Feeling dehydrated, Jane bought a large Dr. Pepper from a concession stand and found shade under a carport. When one of the dragsters started nearby it startled her. She couldn't believe how loud it was. The earth shook under her feet as she covered her ears. She remembered the hearing protection her mother had given her and dug out a pair from of her pocket.

"I need to sit down," she said to Nancy.

"The teams have reserved seats in the grandstand," Nancy said and led the way.

The smell of exhaust hit Jane like a ton of bricks, and she felt like she was going to be sick. They made their way over, and sitting down made Jane feel better. She washed down another couple of Advil with her Dr. Pepper and chewed on the ice.

That's when she noticed the man with the horn-rimmed glasses.

He took a seat near them and appeared to have his eye on her. Jane got the impression he had followed them to their seats. When an usher standing in the aisle asked him for his credentials it was clear the man didn't have a lanyard. The usher pointed him to the general admission seating, and the man obliged, but not before glancing at Jane one more time.

"Do you know that guy?" Jane asked her mother, pointing him out.

"No."

"He was checking me out."

"Because you're my beautiful daughter," she said with pride.

The horn-rimmed man talked to another man wearing a green visor. The man with the visor gave her look before they both blended into the crowd. Jane lost sight of them. She wondered if they were a threat, or if her lingering sickness was making her even more paranoid. She reached into her purse and adjusted the Colt Mustang into position for an easy draw.

After the announcer came on, welcoming race fans and reporting changes in the program, all stood for the national anthem. Her mother put her hand over her heart, and Jane mimicked her. During the last verse three parachutists appeared above them in the sky, each parachute the

American flag. Red, white and blue smoke streamed from pods strapped to each of their ankles. All three landed in unison to roaring applause.

Two "funny cars" were introduced at the starting line. These were different from Danny's car. They had a stock car body and Jane asked her mother why they call them funny cars. She didn't know.

By the time the engines were warmed up, and the cars had burned tires back and forth at the starting line, Jane knew she couldn't take an entire day of this. The bank of lights between the cars cued the start. The dragsters blazed down the stretch. Even though Jane had protection, she still had to hold her hands over her ears. It was loud.

She suffered through a half dozen races until Danny's car was up. Jane could see he was dressed in a fire-retardant suit and thought it must be really hot wearing that thing. A few of the crew joined her and her mother in the grandstands. She could see Danny pull on his helmet and climb into the dragster.

Side by side, he and the dragster he was set to run against burned rubber preparing for the race. This was a ritual, Jane came to learn, that maximized traction off the line. The acrid smoke wafted into the stands and made Jane cough.

Nancy grabbed her arm. "I get so nervous," she said.

The bank of lights cued, and the dragsters explodeed off the line. Flames jetted from the exhaust pipes and Jane could feel the sonic percussion in her chest. Side by side they thundered down the straightaway. When they reached the finish line, a mere three seconds later, parachutes popped out of the back of each car. It took a long distance to slow down past the finish line.

The crowd cheered with enthusiasm.

When the results lit up the board, Nancy did not appear happy.

"What's the matter?" Jane asked.

"Not the best time," her mother explained. "But it all depends on how the others run."

Everyone walked back to the pit shed. Danny soon met them there with the dragster. As the team descended on the machine, Danny explained, "Clutch failure in the upper gears. We'll get her in the next run." He pulled off his fire-retardant suit and joined the others to work on the car.

Nancy explained the team would rebuild the engine and race again in a few hours. Jane saw the opportunity and proposed she get the keys to Danny's truck so she could take a nap. Her mother was reluctant at first, wanting Jane to stay with them, but then finally agreed. "I'll come get you when we're ready to run again."

Jane figured she had at least an hour to nap.

The walk to Danny's truck was welcome relief from the noise, smoke and commotion. Jane removed the ear protection plugs and put them in her pocket. She climbed in the truck, rolled down the windows a few inches for air, and then adjusted the seat as far back as it would go. She pulled the pistol from her purse and curled up with the Colt just as she had while sleeping in the Chevy on her drive to California.

She closed her eyes and was drifting off when she heard footsteps on gravel. It sounded as if someone was close to the truck. Jane sat up but nobody was there. She scanned her surroundings. Nothing. After a moment she lay back again but kept her ears alert. Other than the racing in the distance, there seemed to be nothing of concern. Jane finally closed her eyes. She figured she may not be able to sleep, but at least she could rest.

Exhaustion won out, and she drifted off.

In her dream came images of Big Sur's dramatic coast. She walked on the beach as waves crashed the jagged rocks around her. Then she came across an old wooden lifeboat full of gold bars. Strange. Beyond it there was a woman sitting at the edge of the water, her back to Jane, weeping. She could see the woman was hunched over a dead child, trying to revive her. The toddler's face was blue. She had drowned, a victim of the *Yankee Blade*.

Jane was startled by a strange sound and awoke. She sat up to see the plastic spout of a gas can wedged into the crack of the truck's passenger side window. Raw gasoline poured inside. Jane screamed.

She went for the driver's side door but it would not budge. Something was blocking it. She put her weight into it without luck. Out the side window she could see a thick strap, the kind used to hold cargo on flatbed trucks, snug over the door. Someone had wrapped this strap beneath the truck and around the top of the cab. Winched tight, it clinched both doors. The pink-colored gasoline streamed inside and the scent hit strong.

Then she saw the man with horn-rimmed glasses standing in front of the truck. He had a propane torch in one hand, the kind used to strip paint, and a Bic lighter in the other. He ignited the torch and adjusted the light blue flame.

Jane screamed again.

She raised her gun and fired through the windshield. The safety glass splintered but other than the fractured hole where the bullet had penetrated the glass remained intact. She couldn't see him beyond the fractured windshield so where had he gone?

She went for the passenger door, pushed the gas can out, and tried that door. It, too, wouldn't budge. The puddle of gas in the seat soaked her linen pants and she could feel the caustic fumes harsh in her throat. Then Jane saw the man in the rearview mirror. He had the propane torch raised.

She stuck the gun out the crack in the window and fired back, but was certain she didn't hit him. The she went for the ignition. The truck started, lurched forward, but there was little room to make the turn. Instead Jane smashed into the back of a SUV.

She was putting Danny's truck in reverse when she saw the man in the sideview mirror. He was closing in and poised to toss the propane torch.

Jane abandoned the wheel and fired through the rear window of the cab. Then she put her feet on the seat and pressed against the glass. Jane broke through at the same time he tossed the propane torch into the cab.

The gasoline ignited. An explosion rocked the truck and blew out the windows.

Sprawled facedown in the truck bed, she could feel the heat on her back. Shards of burning glass scaled the back of her neck. She spun to see the inside of the truck aflame and realized her pants were soaked in gas. A flammable wick, she had to get away.

With the Colt in hand, she jumped from the bed of the truck and ran with all her might. There were gunshots as car windshields shattered beside her.

She turned back and fired but after a few shots was out of bullets. She knew she hadn't hit him so cut through the space between parked cars. She glanced back. He was following.

She ran to the racetrack, the area just beyond the finish line. More gunshots sounded so she zig-zagged—a changing target. She reached the track, hopped over the concrete barrier, then ran across the lane.

She jumped over the middle concrete barrier and found herself on the other track. That's when she heard the engines roar. She kept going and reached the outside but came across a wire fence. She turned back, realized she was trapped as the man moved toward her, adjusting his thick glasses, and took aim.

Then she heard the cars.

He had little time to react. The man stutter-stepped in an attempt to get out of the way but the dragster in his lane was traveling way too fast. It swerved sideways to avoid him, fishtailed at over three hundred miles per hour.

From Jane's perspective, when the dragster struck the man his body split in half. The torso flew skyward while the legs were yanked under the tires. The car slammed into the rail and exploded in a ball of fire.

CHAPTER 12

Jane instinctively ducked behind the concrete barrier and hugged the asphalt. She could hear the crashing metal and the crowd reacting with oohs and ahhs. The announcer barked something she couldn't understand followed by the sound of sirens. Jane sat up but because of the smoke she couldn't see anything.

She knew she had to get out of there. There would be an inquiry and police. The press surely would make a big deal about it. Then Veronica would realize Jane had survived another attempt on her life.

The thought came to her: *fake my own death.*

Danny's burning truck, this wreck, so much carnage nobody would know she was alive unless she stuck around.

There appeared to be room to slide under the wire barricade. As emergency vehicles blew past, Jane crawled on her belly under the fence. The veil of smoke gave her ample cover, a literal smoke-screen. She climbed to her feet and slipped the gun in the front pocket of her linen pants. Getting as far away from the smoke and burning wreckage as she could, Jane stepped on something—shattered horn-rimmed glasses.

What are the chances?

She kicked them aside and made her way upstream against curious onlookers running to the crash. There was a cluster of recreational vehicles. When she got to the encampment it seemed like a ghost town. It appeared most everyone had gone to see the wreck.

Jane realized her purse containing her cell phone, credit card, fake ID, and keys to the Chevy were all in the burning truck and most likely incinerated by now. She did, thankfully, have the key card for the hotel room.

A teenage girl sat in a camping chair, bored, ear buds in and engrossed in her cell phone. It appeared she could not care less about the wreck and was far more interested in the content of her tiny screen.

Jane approached and said, "Excuse me."

The girl looked up.

"My mother is going to be worried sick," she said, thumbing back over her shoulder to the plume of smoke rising in the air, "and I don't have my phone with me. Can I borrow yours to tell her I'm okay?"

The girl sized her up, squinting, and said, "You smell like gas."

"Yeah...an accident."

"You all right?"

"I'm okay."

The girl studied her a moment, got up from the chair. She pulled the earphone jack out and handed the iPhone to her.

"Thank you," Jane said and dialed her mother. It rang and rang. She was afraid she'd have to leave a voicemail, but then Nancy picked up.

"Mom," Jane said. "I'm okay."

"Where are you?"

"Near the wreck, but I'm fine."

"Whose phone are you calling from? I don't recognize the number."

"A really nice girl was kind enough to lend me hers," she said, then stepped away out of earshot. "Mom, listen. That man from the grandstands tried to kill me."

"What man?"

"The one eyeballing me. And he lit Danny's truck on fire."

"What!?"

"He's the reason for this crash."

"They said there was someone on the track... where are you?"

Jane thought about the other guy she saw, the man with the visor she'd seen talking with the horn-rimmed assassin and said, "I don't know if he was alone or if there are more."

"More of who? Jane, are you all right?"

"Veronica got to me through you, Mom. Be careful. Watch your back."

"Meet me in the pit shed."

"I can't."

"Then Danny's truck."

Jane could see the separate plume of smoke coming from where Danny's truck was parked. She said, "I need to get out of here. I'll call you tonight. I love you." She hung up and walked back to the girl. "Thank you," she said and handed the phone back. "My mom will probably call back but you don't have to answer. It's probably better if you don't."

The girl's phone rang. She put it on silence, considered Jane, and said, "You, uh...okay?"

"I'm fine," Jane lied.

"Want water, or something?"

"That would be great."

The girl dug into a nearby cooler and handed Jane a plastic bottle.

"Thank you," Jane said, and twisted off the cap. Water was exactly what she needed at that moment. "Where's your family?" Jane asked.

"Went to see what happened, I guess."

"You're not interested?"

"Crashes scare me."

"Me too," Jane said.

The girl nodded and gave her a smile.

Jane marched on. She'd have to find a way to get back to the hotel and get out of the gas-soaked clothes. She needed a shower before she drove back to Morro Bay.

She remembered what Danny had said to her in his garage in Florida. *Backup* is what he called it. She recalled that after she'd run from Cooper to Danny's shop, and used the hide-a-key to get in, he'd mentioned there was also hide-a-key under the fender of the Chevy. She had never checked for it, but if it was true the muscle car would be her getaway.

Jane marched toward the highway, determined to get back to the hotel. She planned to stand on the side of the road with her thumb out.

CHAPTER 13

The scrawny trucker didn't ask Jane why she smelled like gasoline. By the time he'd pulled over to pick her up most of the gas had evaporated out of her clothes, but she could still smell it on her skin. The scent made her queasy.

Hitchhiking seemed so old fashioned, like from a bad '70s movie, but she had no choice. The moment after the tractor trailer pulled over, Jane hesitated. *Is this a good idea?* But the gun gave her confidence even though she was out of bullets.

Once she climbed into the truck she could see the lean trucker was more interested in talking about Christian values than anything else. She said little but encouraged with silent nods. In the half hour it took to drive Jane to the hotel, she learned his life story, once a wayward son of sin and debauchery before he was born again. He used the word "repent" just as she had with Danny the night before.

Repent.

When he dropped her off in front of the hotel, the trucker handed Jane a pamphlet for his on-line church. "God Bless, sister," were his parting words.

Jane thanked him, and after he drove off the first

thing she did was check under the Chevy's fender for the hide-a-key. There was nothing. She tried the other wheel wells but it wasn't there either. Tears of frustration came to her eyes but she fought them off, knew she needed to stay focused. She went back to the front wheel well and tried again. She felt around inside. Sure enough Jane came across the magnetized, metallic case and pulled it out. Inside there was a spare key and folded twenty dollar bill.

She showered quickly and got dressed. The only thing clean to wear was the mini dress so it would have to do. There was second magazine for the Colt in her suitcase. When she swapped out the spent clip for the new one, Jane could smell the burnt gunpowder on the weapon. She left a note for her mother letting her know she'd taken the Chevy, then set out.

Her plan was to take the direct route down Highway 101 back to Morro Bay. Without her trusty credit card, she hoped there was enough gas in the tank to make it. The twenty dollar bill came in handy at a Chevron in Salinas. By the time she pulled into Morro Bay the needle on the fuel gauge was below empty.

When they last spoke, Cooper had mentioned he was staying in a motel close enough to spy on the yacht. Jane had no problem finding the place. Although it was getting dark, it was obvious what room he was in by the binoculars mounted on a tripod visible outside the second floor balcony. She found a small stone and threw it at the sliding glass door. After a moment Cooper emerged. "You're back," he said.

"She tried to kill me."

He motioned her to come up.

In the darkened motel room, Jane explained how she had barely escaped with her life.

"I don't think he was alone. There had to be others," she said with images in her mind of both the flat-nosed intruder she'd battled in Florida and the man in horn-rimmed glasses.

"Veronica probably put a bounty on your head," he said.

"A bounty?"

"The first man to kill you collects the prize."

"So there will be more?"

"As long as she's around to pay the bounty hunters." He explained that there had been much activity around the boat. "The crew no longer goes home at night. They're now sleeping on the boat."

"Any sign of Veronica?"

"No."

She obsessed on the thought of hired assassins and wondered how much Veronica offered for her, dead or alive.

For most of the evening Jane watched the yacht from the balcony. Cabin lights were on, and there was little activity up on deck. It reminded her of the night she saw Cooper's yacht docked in Marina Del

Rey. Her neighbor Carla had driven her, and that night she had seen him on his boat with another woman. Although Jane didn't realize it at the time, she knew now it was Veronica. Jane thought back on it. So much had happened so fast.

Cooper learned there were no other rooms available in the motel. Since there was only one bed in the room, without saying a word he took a pillow and blanket and made an impromptu bed on the floor. Jane was grateful and it put her at ease. He was holding up his end of the bargain. It wasn't that long ago, she thought, that the two of them had been lovers. She recalled the moments they shared and the feel of his embrace. She wondered what her life would be like if she had never met him and had never agreed to be his shill. Why hadn't she had the common sense to run the other way when he confessed he was a criminal? But no, she didn't. Because she loved him? *Love is blind,* she lamented, head on her pillow.

She couldn't sleep, and Cole Porter's tune "I've Got You Under My Skin" came to mind. Sinatra had made it universally popular but she favored Diana Krall's slow tempo version. Jane loved Cole Porter's songs, and this was one her favorites. His tunes all tended to be love stories with great irony. Thanks to Cole Porter, she had been caught in a double entendre having a drink with Gallagher in the Plaza Hotel with the lyrics to "Let's Misbehave." And then the band on Veronica's secluded island played "Love For Sale." Jane had memorized the lyrics to "I've Got You Under My Skin" long ago, and lying in bed the melody played in her head. One verse went, "I'd sacrifice anything come what might, for the sake of having you near, in spite of a warning voice that comes in the night, and repeats in my ear."

Of course the "warning voice" that "comes at night" and "repeats in my ear."

A *warning voice* was there when she first met Cooper. Jane realized she'd ignored it. The song continued in her head, "You can never win. Use your mentality...wake up to reality." Cole Porter had true wisdom and she wished she had taken it to heart.

Lights out, she heard him stir on the floor and wondered if Cooper would try to join her in bed. It didn't look like he was going to, but if he did Jane figured she wouldn't necessarily resist as wrong as it may be.

He kept his word. That was best.

After a while, she heard him begin to snore. She'd remembered it from the evenings they'd spent together, her lying in bed after he was asleep. Jane knew that Veronica was familiar with Cooper's snore too and wondered what she thought of it. This was the man they had both loved.

Or was Veronica capable of love?

CHAPTER 14

The next morning Jane heard Cooper get up. He tossed his blanket and went into the bathroom. She hadn't slept well. When she got up to peer out the window Jane was surprised to see much activity around Brendan's yacht. "Something's going on," she said.

Cooper emerged from the bathroom and peered through the binoculars. "Looks like they're getting ready to shove off."

"A day early?"

"We've got to make sure Veronica's on that boat."

They got dressed quickly, jumped in the rental car, and drove down the hill. Cooper parked on Embarcadero, the closest they'd ever been to the yacht. She could see Brendan supervising others as they brought provisions on board.

"I don't see Veronica," Jane said.

"She'll be here."

"What if she doesn't come?"

"She has to."

As if on cue, a black Audi with tinted windows pulled into the parking lot. Brendan walked from the gangway, went to the driver's side window, and was engaged in conversation with someone inside the vehicle.

"Could that be her?" Jane asked.

Cooper was silent.

Then the driver's side door opened and Billy came running out. Jane could see Cooper tense at the sight of the boy and raise the binoculars for a closer look. His son ran around the parking lot then went to the railing to look at the yacht.

"That's Billy," Jane said, stating the obvious.

"Then it's definitely her."

Sure enough, Veronica emerged from the sedan. Jane could see she was dressed in black active wear as if she was going on a run or joining a yoga class. The last time Jane had seen Veronica she had slipped under the waves in the Caribbean. Now here she was—the proud descendant of pirate Anne Bonny about to board another boat.

She and Brendan spoke. There were nods and gestures before Brendan turned and barked orders to the crew. Veronica returned to the sedan and grabbed a small backpack. She went to the energetic Billy, kneeled down, and hugged her son as if he was heading off to camp. He shouldered his backpack and ran for the boat.

"Where's her bag?" Jane said.

Cooper said nothing. Then as Veronica stood on the dock, the *Maenads* shoved off, her son on board.

"Why isn't she going with them?" Jane asked.

"I don't get it," Cooper said softly.

Jane realized Cooper's scheme would only work if Veronica was on that boat—the yacht with the stashed missile launcher.

"What do we do?" Jane asked.

She could see Cooper was at a complete loss, his face pale. His carefully crafted plan had just crumbled before his eyes.

Jane said, "Start the car."

He simply blinked.

"Follow her," Jane demanded. She could see Veronica get into the sedan and pull out of the parking lot. "Don't get too close," Jane said.

The sedan headed out, and they followed. It swerved its way into a turn lane.

"Don't lose her!"

A flustered Cooper maneuvered the rental car to keep up. Jane felt as if she had to steer the ship now and tell *him* what to do. *What was the matter? Had he gone soft at the sight of his son?*

They followed Veronica as she weaved onto Highway 1 toward San Luis Obispo.

"If she's not supervising from the yacht, then where could she be going?" asked Jane, hoping to bring Cooper back to a tactical mindset.

"Why would she bring Billy along?" he wondered.

"She wants him with her when it's time to escape," she said.

After a fifteen minute drive, Veronica reached

San Luis Obispo and pulled into the parking lot of the Amtrak station and parked. Cooper, keeping their distance, found a spot on the street. Jane checked out the California vintage depot with its signature Mission Revival architecture—stucco exterior and red clay tile roof before Veronica got out and walked to the station.

"The Amtrak Pacific Surfliner," Jane remembered, "the tracks cut through the base."

"But the train doesn't stop there."

"Close to it, right?"

"There's a seasonal stop at Surf Station in Lompoc, but that's miles north of Point Arguello."

"Let me see your phone."

He punched his code and handed it over. Jane searched. She pulled up a map and pointed it out, "Look, the tracks hug the coast and cross between Point Arguello and the launch facility."

Veronica emerged from the train station, ticket in hand, and returned to the sedan. At first Jane thought she was wearing yoga pants, but on closer inspection it appeared to be flat black triathlete clothing. Her tight compression clothing glistened in the sun. She opened the trunk, hoisted a sleek backpack on her shoulder, pulled dark sunglasses down, and walked to the platform. If there was ever a time that Veronica looked like a black widow, Jane thought, this was it.

"We've got to get on that train," Jane said.

"She'll see us."

He was right. There was little room on the concrete platform and no way they could stand there without Veronica noticing them.

"What's the next station south?" she asked.

He consulted his phone, "Grover Beach."

"She might not see us board there."

Jane could see the concept dawn on Cooper's hardened face. "Let's do it."

They sped south on Highway 101, past Pismo Beach, and pulled into the parking lot of the Grover Beach Amtrak station. This unmanned station, also Mission Revival, simply offered shelter and a seating area considerably more modest compared to the San Luis Obispo depot. Jane strapped on her purse and felt the weight of the Colt on her shoulder. Cooper grabbed his shoulder bag and pulled on a baseball cap. She grabbed the pocket umbrella from the back seat of the car.

At the electronic kiosk Cooper bought a pair of tickets as Jane found cover behind a Spanish-tile pillar. There were a dozen people waiting, evidence the train would be there soon. The idea came to her, and she said, "I wonder if the Air Force base runs everyone on the yacht through a check point."

"And taking the train Veronica avoids that," he said, finishing her thought.

"Exactly."

"She's obsessed with not leaving a paper trail so that makes sense. But nobody can get off the train on restricted government land."

"Unless someone pulls the emergency brake and jumps off," Jane ventured.

Cooper snapped, pointed to Jane and said, "You figured it out."

"We'll see," she said.

A train horn sounded. Jane could see the Pacific Surfliner round the bend up ahead. Veronica was on that train.

CHAPTER 15

Jane and Cooper waited behind the pillar of the Grover Beach station until the Pacific Surfliner slowed to a stop, brakes screeching. Jane popped up the umbrella in the event Veronica was seated on the right side of the train. Only one of the train's car doors opened and two conductors jumped out. One set a stepstool on the concrete platform. The other shouted, "All aboard."

Jane and Cooper shared the cover of the umbrella and moved to the train car. Once on board, Jane directed Cooper to seats nearby. Hunched low, she whispered, "We need to find Veronica without being seen. If she's seated in the cars ahead we can approach from behind, no problem. But if she's seated in the cars behind us she'll see us come through the car door."

"We need a disguise," Cooper said.

Jane racked her brain.

"Tickets?" the grey haired conductor said.

He punched them, tore off a piece of each, then wedged the receipt into the clip on the side of the seat.

"Where's the bar car?" Jane asked.

"Up ahead, ma'am," he said and moved on.

"I'll go forward first," she said, "and see if she's ahead of us."

"I'll go."

"No, she'll recognize you before she does me."

"She'll be on the right side," he said.

"How do you know?"

"It's got the ocean view."

"Makes sense," Jane took the baseball cap off Cooper's head and put it on her own. She dug sunglasses out of her purse. Not the greatest disguise, but it would have to do. She got up and entered the forward car, moving cautiously, upstream against a few passengers carrying cardboard concession trays coming from the bar car.

Veronica wasn't in the next car, so she moved on. In the vestibule between cars the deck rocked and Jane almost lost her balance. She took a moment to consider the hatch below on the diamond-plate deck. A hinged metal door allowed access to drop down to the tracks. She assumed that was how Veronica planned to get off.

Up ahead in the next car she saw the back of a brunette and drew close. Jane could see it was Veronica by the way she moved her head, like a cat: precise and graceful. She was sitting alone at a window staring out at the ocean, lost in thought. Jane wondered what was on her mind as she stepped even closer. A mere fifteen feet away, Jane could see Veronica held an electronic device in her hand. Jane recognized it as a GPS device.

She backed off but something else caught her eye. Not far, on the train bulkhead, the red latch for the emergency brake. She'd chosen her seat wisely.

CHAPTER 16

She showed Cooper the hatch between the train cars and they made their plan before they settled in and waited. When there were no homes or commercial structures in sight it was obvious the train had crossed onto Vandenberg Air Force Base, the landscape barren with low scrub. There were occasional buildings scattered here and there and Jane noticed large white towers. Upon closer inspection, she could see "Titan II" in black text on the side of one of them. She had read about these, the defunct launch pads. There were others that appeared fully operational.

"Once we get off the train we have to stay out of sight," Cooper said. "Air Force Security will probably respond to a stopped train. If we're caught we're going to jail, no questions asked."

"So once Veronica gets on the boat," she asked, "that's when you'll call?"

"You wanted to witness the perp walk? Now you'll see her arrest."

Jane had been meaning to ask him, and said, "You were married to her. Did you ever pick up on her treachery and second guess your decision?"

"Many times."

"But you stayed with her."

"We had a child together. If you want to understand think of it this way, Veronica is a cheat."

"A cheat?"

"She lives to cheat. She cheated in our marriage...hell she cheats playing cards. It's her nature. She can't help it. If she put the same effort into honest work Veronica could have been very successful. But she can't help herself."

They sat in silence for the rest of the trip. After a while Jane felt the train go around a slight bend. Then it finally happened. An electronic alarm sounded and the train came to an abrupt halt. The conductor ran past them into the next car, his radio squawking.

"Now," Jane said.

She grabbed the ticket receipts out of the seat and, for the benefit of the passengers around them, Jane said, "I can use a drink." She asked him, "You buying?"

On the spot, Cooper stammered for a moment before he said "Sure." She and Cooper went to the sliding door and entered the vestibule.

Through the window in the forward door they could see the conductor and waited until the he'd moved into the car ahead. Then she gave Cooper a nod. He pulled up the hatch and they dropped down to the tracks. She made sure to replace the hatch so it wasn't obvious they'd jumped off before they hid beside the train wheels.

Jane could see Veronica move out from below the train car ahead and, unbeknownst that they were there, she scrambled down into a ravine and darted into a corrugated metal drain tunnel buried beneath the tracks.

She heard the conductor open the side door near them and saw his legs drop down. Ducking low, they moved to hide in the space near the train wheels. She was so close her bare arm brushed against the wheel and Jane burnt herself. She suppressed the pain, gritting her teeth. She had no idea it would be so hot.

It appeared as if the conductor was searching for signs that someone got off the train, and another conductor met him. They conversed for a moment and then ducked underneath to examine the other side.

Jane saw the window of opportunity. Much like the tunnel Veronica had found, there was a similar one behind them. Since the conductors couldn't see them now, she said to Cooper, "Follow me."

They ducked into the dirt ravine and wriggled into the corrugated tunnel, barely wide enough to fit them both. It was muddy inside with spider webs and standing water. Jane wiped the webs from her face and pressed on. It smelled like something had died in there.

The proximity to Cooper felt awkward. This was the closest she'd been to him since they'd last slept together. She distanced herself as much as she could.

Just as Cooper had predicted, from their vantage point they could see a pair of Humvee vehicles arrive and a half dozen men of the Air Force 30th Security Forces Squadron jump out. The soldiers were dressed in full khaki camouflage and wore dark blue berets. A few carried M-4 carbines. She had been so focused on chasing Veronica she hadn't even thought about how they'd get off the base.

The commander spoke with one of the conductors as the others did their reconnaissance. Jane was certain they would look in the tunnels, but nobody did. After a few minutes, the conductors climbed back on the train and it continued on its way. The soldiers returned to their vehicles, took a moment to radio in their findings, and then departed. After they had gone, Cooper went to the end of the tunnel and pointed out a small airplane in the sky above them. "UAV," he whispered.

"What's that?"

"Unmanned Aerial Vehicle," he said.

"A drone?"

"It might circle for a while. We may have to wait until dark."

"What about Veronica?"

Jane peaked out to consider Veronica's tunnel. It appeared she, too, was laying low.

"We have to be quiet," Cooper said in a hushed

tone. “This tunnel amplifies everything, like a horn.”

She could see he was right and tried to settle in while keeping an eye on Veronica’s tunnel. She concentrated on her breathing to slow her heart-rate.

The afternoon dragged on and there was no movement as Veronica stayed hidden. Jane grew thirsty and wished she’d brought water. At one point she heard another train approach but it was unclear which direction it was heading. As it passed overhead she assumed it was northbound from the echo but couldn’t see it to confirm.

Still, Veronica did not emerge.

Jane began to wonder if Veronica had slipped away without them seeing her, but then she saw her arm at the end of the tunnel tossing a wrapper out. Jane ducked back, and by the time she ventured another look she could see a silver wrapper blowing in the wind. The breeze brought the wrapper past and Jane could see it was a power bar. Veronica had come prepared. She had snacks, and probably water. *Damn.*

It was hot and Jane was so thirsty she considered sipping the standing water pooled in the corrugated pipe but knew that would only make her sick.

The wait was interminable.

At one point Cooper fell asleep. His snoring was so loud she had to wake him.

Two hours later another train passed. That one

was clearly heading north and she wished she could jump on board and get a bottle of water from the bar car. Wasn't there a Johnny Cash song, she remembered, something about a prisoner yearning for freedom and every time the train passed by out his prison window it tortured him? Didn't the guy imagine passengers at ease sipping coffee and smoking cigars? She'd heard the song played in Danny's truck.

As dusk arrived Jane was even more vigilant in watching Veronica's tunnel so she wouldn't miss her. Finally, only after the sky had transformed from sunset gold to a dark blue, Veronica emerged.

"She's out," whispered Jane.

She and Cooper watched as Veronica stretched her muscles as if she'd just awakened from a nap. She sipped bottled water, gave the area a once over, then moved toward the coastal cliffs.

"Where's she going?" Jane whispered.

"To the yacht," Cooper said.

CHAPTER 17

Keeping a safe distance, Jane and Cooper followed Veronica. They took cover behind scrub brush as she made her way to the cliffs. Jane could see Brendan's yacht tied to a military vessel, gunmetal grey with clusters of antennas.

"Security running background checks," Cooper said.

Jane's lips were cracked and her throat parched from thirst. Meanwhile Veronica casually sipped water at the bluff. It was driving Jane crazy.

The military vessel pulled up anchor and powered away and Veronica got a phone call. Only then did she drop down from the cliffs to the beach below.

Jane and Cooper snuck up closer.

Veronica stashed her backpack on a cluster of rocks and then started to wade into the ocean. Jane realized why Veronica had chosen triathlon wear. "She's swimming out to the yacht," she said.

"Of course she is," Cooper said.

Jane remembered the framed photo of teenage Veronica adorned with gold swim medals. She'd seen the photo in Veronica's bedroom on Stingray Cay. Then, before Veronica got away, she snatched the framed picture. Jane wondered where the photo was now.

Although the sun had long set over the water, Veronica was backlit by the lingering light in the sky. She swam past the whitewash, her strokes graceful. Jane could see Veronica had the kind of athletic form only expert training buys. Much like an elegant tennis forehand, or perfect golf swing, you know it when you see it. There are some things not learned in public pools or city parks, where Jane had spent her youth. Veronica had come from a life of privilege and learned to swim at country club pools. So where did it all go wrong?

When Veronica reached the boat Jane could see Billy at the railing. Brendan and the crew tossed a rope ladder and assisted her on board. They had a towel waiting for the boss.

"Call base security," she said to Cooper.

"Tomorrow."

"But she's on the boat."

"After they dig up the gold."

"When did you decide that?"

"Just now."

"I'm not sticking around. Call them."

"Jane..."

"Besides, I'm dying of thirst here."

"I bet there's water in the backpack she left behind."

"This is crazy," Jane said, getting angry. "Call now and they'll turn that boat back around."

"There's no rush."

"We can't be here. Soldiers will find us. We'll be the ones arrested."

"There are caves in these cliffs we can hide in."

"Fuck that!" Jane said. She pulled the Colt from her purse. "I'm not staying around here. Get this over with. Call in the cavalry."

"Let's get some water and talk about it."

She aimed the .380 at his chest. "There's nothing to talk about. We had a deal."

He just looked at her before he said, "We can't risk it at night. That boat comes back and Veronica will jump back in the water. Nobody will see her at night, and she'll disappear again."

There was a degree of logic in that. Jane remembered the night she'd survived the wreck of the *Anne Bonny*. She was certain Veronica went down with the ship but the darkness of the night allowed her to swim away unseen.

Suddenly she heard a loud crack followed by a thunderous noise. They both turned to the source, a rocket launching. The earth rumbled beneath Jane's feet and she couldn't believe her eyes. The night instantly turned to day as the flaming contrail pulsated below the climbing projectile. She'd seen this sort of thing on TV but the sight of it so close was jaw dropping. As the rocket continued to climb and arch toward the ocean Jane heard cheers coming from the yacht. It was as if this was a firework show for their benefit.

"Did you know they were going to do that?" she asked Cooper.

He appeared as amazed as she. "No."

Jane swallowed hard. "Let's get that water."

CHAPTER 18

Under the cover of darkness they descended the cliffs and Jane found Veronica's backpack on the rocks. There were two bottles of Fiji water, one of them half gone. Jane took the unopened bottle and tossed Cooper the other. He could drink Veronica's backwash. *Hell, aren't they still married?*

"There's something I didn't tell you," he said.

"Now what?"

"I told you the truth, just not the whole truth."

"What a surprise," she said with sarcasm.

"Listen, there's not going to be a lot of prospecting and time wasted. These guys she brought in are going to have to dig, for sure, but Veronica has a pretty good idea where the gold is buried. She's been here before."

"When?"

"Both of us were here years ago, posing as surfers. We snuck in by boat, dug up a few gold coins in a collapsed cave right over there," he said pointing, "but only reached the tip of the iceberg before we were caught. This was before they ramped up security, before domestic terrorism and drones."

"So this is not about revenge for your brother's

death, it's about padding your bankroll," she said.

"It's about getting my son back with a nest egg to ensure he'll grow up right and be a better person than me."

Jane lamented, "All this is nothing but a family squabble, and I'm the sap in the middle of it."

"It's about stopping Veronica for good."

"Give me that phone," she demanded, gun raised.

"I'll throw it in the waves, I swear to God," he threatened, and held it up as if he were to toss it.

"Don't be ridiculous."

"Give me until morning," he pleaded. "And I'll split what we find fifty-fifty."

"You'll burn me again."

"I swear on my son's life...I can't hide from you, Jane. You're too smart, and too good. You found Veronica, and you'd definitely find me." He looked out to the yacht. "Think about it, this gold could be a leg up. You want to be a waitress in your old age?"

"I'm an actress!"

"Same thing."

"I don't care about money," she snapped with anger. "I just want my life back."

"Twenty-four hours. That's all I ask. Tomorrow night Veronica will be in jail and you'll be sipping a fine cabernet at the Biltmore in Santa Barbara."

"How do you plan to get the gold out of here?" she questioned.

"Once Veronica uncovers the cave we call in the Air Force. We wait until they're all arrested and hauled away, and then move in. Maybe we stash it in that tunnel under the tracks for now and come back later."

"And where do we hide?"

He pointed. "The caves in those cliffs. Nobody will be able to see us there."

Once again Jane realized she was at a crossroads. On one hand she considered shooting him in the leg, grabbing the phone, and calling the authorities herself. But on the other hand something tugged her the other way—impulse. In the end the fear of Veronica getting away in the darkness is what swayed her most. She'd come too far. She couldn't let Veronica slip away a second time.

"Show me," she said.

CHAPTER 19

Jane sat on a ledge under the overhang, gun in hand. The caves Cooper spoke of were nothing more than deep crevices within the cliffs. The one they were huddled in, the deepest, barely offered cover from the wind. She'd spotted a bat swoop past them, and it was getting cold. She said, "I'm going to freeze to death."

He slipped off his dark fleece REI pullover and gave it to her.

"What about you?" she said.

"I'll be fine."

She put the pullover on and sat on the ground. She curled up and stretched it over her knees, like she'd when she was younger. There was something metallic in the front pocket. Jane pulled it out—a pair of handcuffs.

"What the...?" she said.

He said nothing.

She pointed the gun at him, handcuffs in the other hand. "Are these supposed to be for me?"

"Of course not. Veronica."

"You've been carrying these around everywhere so when the time is right you plan on locking me to something to make your escape."

"That's not true," he said.

"Why do you have handcuffs?"

"Like I said, for Veronica."

"I don't believe you."

"Keep them. I don't care."

Jane said. "What's that saying? Fool me once..."

"Believe what you want. Those aren't for you."

They sat for a long time in silence. Finally Cooper broke the ice explaining where the gold was buried, inside a cave wall in a lagoon-shaped canyon within the cliffs. "At low tide you can enter the lagoon at sea level, but only for an hour or two before the waves make it impossible as the sea rises. The only way to get to it is to repel down from above."

Jane could hear music coming from the anchored yacht, its cabin lights glistening off the black water. Occasionally laughter echoed. "They're having a party," Jane said.

"And nobody realizes this is their last night of freedom."

Jane imagined what it must have been like for the survivors of the *Yankee Blade*. Maybe passengers fortunate enough to come ashore found shelter in this very same cave. She came to the conclusion that pure greed was ultimately the culprit, whether it be from Captain Randall or Veronica, unbridled greed is what bought on so much misery.

The hours dragged on and she spent the night watching both Cooper and Brendan's yacht. The distant wails of seals accompanied the pre-dawn light, much like birds welcoming a new day. Cooper decided to empty Veronica's backpack. There was a single power bar, peanut butter. He broke it in half, offered the meager ration to Jane, and said, "Breakfast."

She shook her head no.

Even before the sun was up the crew had inflatable boats aside the yacht and Veronica led the team ashore. Her son Billy was with them. Hidden back in the shadow of the cave, Jane could see Veronica go to where she had stashed the backpack and appeared confused why it wasn't there. Veronica looked down and studied the sand.

"She sees our footprints," Jane whispered.

The high tide had cleared some of their tracks away, but not all. Veronica scanned the beach. Jane ducked back further into the cave. "Get back," she said to Cooper. Laying in the dirt, they both watched as Veronica gave the cliffs a once-over. She held her gaze in their direction and Jane couldn't tell if she'd seen them. It didn't look like she had.

Getting back to business, Veronica tightened a sheath strapped to her leg. It appeared to be a diving knife.

Meanwhile Brendan and his men shuttled cases and equipment from the yacht. They all converged around a canyon wall. Pounding ocean waves crashed the rocks at the base of the crevice. The violent waves appeared to guard the entrance, nature's sentry at the castle gates. Cooper was right. The cave they had chosen was a good spot. They were close enough to see everything, but hidden in the shadows as to not be noticed.

With Veronica supervising, Brendan and his men built aluminum Speed-Rail and scaffolding at the top of the cliff. With a series of ropes they eased it down inside the canyon wall. At one point, a Coast Guard helicopter flew up the shoreline, low over the water. The men on the cliff paused for a moment, then went back to work after it had passed.

Jane could see Billy was bored by all of this. He began wandering up and down the coast, searching for seashells and skipping rocks in the surf. He found a piece of driftwood as a walking stick, poked at seaweed, and began exploring the rocks.

He was coming their way.

"Shit," Jane said. They both scrambled back into the cave.

Billy came closer. If he continued on his path he'd come directly to them, and sure enough, Billy did. The boy was startled and about to call out but Cooper cut him off with, "Billy! It's me."

The boy squinted at them.

"It's Dad," Cooper said. "Come here."

Jane saw recognition on the boy's face. He dropped his walking stick and came running, "Dad!"

They hugged. Cooper said, "We're playing hide

and seek. Don't say anything to anyone."

"Where have you been?" Billy asked.

"In Canada. I missed you so much."

"Mom said you guys had a big fight and you left us."

"I'm back now. Everything is going to be all right. I came back for you."

For the first time ever Jane saw Cooper emotional. He had always been so cool and collected, so in control. But now hugging his son, she could see, Cooper was nothing more than your average, run-of-the-mill father with prideful tears in his eyes.

Billy looked to Jane with caution and said, "Who are you?"

"That's Jane, Billy. She's Mom's friend."

Mom's friend? Jane thought. *There could be nothing farther from the truth.*

"Listen," Cooper said to him, "You can't say anything or you'll ruin our game. Can you keep a secret?"

He nodded.

At that moment Jane heard Veronica call out, "Billy?" She looked to see Veronica walking the shoreline.

"Shh," Cooper said to Billy, pulling him back. "Don't give us away."

"Billy?" Veronica continued, "Where are you, honey?"

Billy played along as Veronica searched. Jane

could see Veronica was growing increasingly agitated.

"Billy!?" Veronica called, now with anger. "Come here right now or you're getting a spanking!"

Jane could see Billy flinch.

"Do you hear me? Come out right now or I'll pull down your pants and spank you in front of everyone! Is that what you want?!"

Jane could see Billy's face turn red. *Does Veronica do that?* From the look in the boy's face Jane could tell it wasn't the physical pain that he feared, but the shame and humiliation. That's what put him over the top.

Billy broke from Cooper and screamed, "Mom?!"

Oh shit. She turned to Cooper and said, "Call now."

He reached in his pocket for his phone, punched up his contacts, then said, "No bars."

"What?"

"Because we're in this cave. I've got to get up on the cliff."

Jane saw Billy run to his mother. He pointed back at them. Although she couldn't hear what he was saying, it was clear the boy was giving them up. *What's that kid's problem? Such a brat.* Jane wondered what he was saying to her, that he'd just seen his father? Veronica would doubt it, wouldn't she? She'd killed Cooper in Dana Point, or so she thought. Jane wondered what she was thinking at that moment as a confused Veronica squinted in their direction. She had a bitter look of concern on her face. Then she violently yanked the boy by the arm and dragged him back to the others.

Cooper ran from the cave and scrambled up the cliff embankment. Jane followed. It was steep and the gravel was loose. Jane kept sliding back and her progress was slow. She looked back over her shoulder and could see Brendan with a rifle coming their way. Jane realized had Cooper chosen another route up the steep cliff, with solid footing, they would have been up the embankment and out of sight by the time the men were there. But it was too late to turn back now and choose another path.

She heard the crack of rifle fire. Clods of dirt exploded beside her. Jane considered firing back but realized the short barrel Colt would be useless at this distance. A rock beside her cracked followed by the ping of a ricochet.

Cooper reached the top first. He reached back to help her as gunfire erupted on either side of them. Jane screamed. He dropped to one knee and pulled her up. She thought it miraculous they hadn't been hit.

Atop the crest, Jane ran for her life. It would take some time for Veronica and her men to climb the cliff. She figured they had a brief window of opportunity.

Jane could see, beyond the train tracks, there

was a cluster of white buildings around the perimeter of the launch pad. *Make it there.*

She ran faster than Cooper as he struggled to keep up. She crossed over the train tracks, ran through dried weeds, and came upon the pavement. The buildings appeared abandoned. Jane went for the closest one. The door was open and she burst in. It was a dark, abandoned machine shop. Rows of lathes and drill presses lined the walls. Cooper followed her in, gulping for air.

"Call," she said.

Catching his breath, Cooper punched his phone. "This is an emergency. Vandenberg Air Force Base Space Launch Complex 8. There is a FIM-92 Stinger missile in the engine room of the boat anchored there." As he gave details over the phone Jane could see his shirt bloody, seeping from his side. His knees gave way and he dropped. She realized he'd been hit, probably when he turned back to helped her up the cliff.

In panic, Jane glanced out the door.

Veronica and her men were closing in.

She pulled the Colt .380 Mustang, chambered a round, and fired.

CHAPTER 20

Even though the Colt Mustang had limited accuracy at that distance, the sound of gunfire gave them pause. Veronica and her men stopped advancing on them and returned fire. Jane and Cooper dropped to the floor as bullets punched through the tin building in a deafening deluge—a hailstorm of lead just above their heads. Shafts of light now pierced the darkness.

Throughout the chaos Cooper continued to give coordinates to someone on the other end of the phone. Through the door Jane could see Brendan advance commando style and she remembered when he recounted his Navy SEAL days. She fired to keep him at bay, but stopped herself when she realized her pistol only held six rounds. She'd have to conserve. Jane thought she'd fired four already. With all the confusion maybe it was five.

She could see Veronica give orders before the team retreated. They moved past the dried weeds towards the cliffs. Soon they were out of sight, and it fell silent. Once Jane felt it was safe, she went over to Cooper and saw a puddle of blood had formed beside him. She yanked off the fleece pullover and held it against his wound.

"Bastards!" he said, clearly in pain.

Applying pressure, the pullover helped control the bleeding. She said, "The cavalry is coming, right?"

"They asked a lot of questions before I lost them. Let's hope they won't write me off as some crazy," he said.

"They'll be here," she said, trying to be positive. "Hang in there."

He looked to her and said, "I'm sorry...I'm sorry I made you my shill. You're a better person than any of us, me, Veronica, all these lowlifes."

Jane said. "What did they say on the phone?"

"I'm sorry. I shouldn't have used you in our scheme. But then I broke rule number one and fell in love." Jane could hear more gunfire in the distance as Cooper continued, "No matter what happens, just know it wasn't my idea to frame you for Wolff's murder back in L.A. That was all Veronica's idea plan. I fought her on it, but this was her caper from the very beginning."

"We'll get you to a hospital." Jane was making progress with his wound, having stopped the bleeding, before she saw his eyes look past her for a second. Then she felt a presence. Before Jane could turn something hard struck her in the back of the head. Her chin hit the concrete and she bit her tongue.

She rolled over to see Brendan standing over her. He'd struck her with the butt of his rifle. Brendan kicked her pistol away, turned to Cooper, and said, "What the fuck, bro? Bring along a nurse?"

How had he snuck up on her? Jane wondered. There must have been a door at the back of the building. The pain was overwhelming and her sight began to blur. There was the taste of blood in her mouth and it felt like she'd bit her tongue in half. She felt nauseous and was certain she was going to throw up.

To Jane, Brendan said, "You were a plant all along, weren't you, bitch?" He tilted his head and said, "And I thought you liked me."

Jane couldn't speak, checked her tongue, it was still intact. She looked in vain for her gun on the floor.

"Brendan," Cooper said through clinched teeth, "Listen to me. Veronica will betray you."

"Dude," he said, "this doesn't concern you."

"You think she's going to split that gold? She cut me out, and she'll do the same to you."

At that point gunfire erupted somewhere in the distance and Brendan went to the door to see.

"Security Forces," Cooper said. "They know who you are."

"We'll see about that," Brendan said, his rifle poised to go into battle.

From the darkness behind them Veronica appeared.

Jane recoiled back. She must have come through the back door too.

Veronica sized both of them up before she turned to Cooper, eyeing him, and said, "Christ almighty...I thought I'd taken care of you. I could have sworn I slit your throat."

"That was my brother," Cooper said, "You killed him by mistake, and now you're fucked."

"Speak for yourself," she said before turning to Jane. "And you, Jane? Do you know how much money I've spent trying to get rid of you? The exterminators I've hired? You're like a cat with nine lives."

Jane remained silent and eyed Veronica with hatred.

"I planted a missile on Brendan's yacht," Cooper said with a hint of pride in his voice. "So it's only a matter of time."

"A what?" Veronica questioned.

"In the engine room, a surface-to-air missile. Security Forces know all about it, and they're on their way."

Brendan put two and two together and said, "You're framing us for treason."

Jane considered that for a second then snapped, "He's bluffing."

"You're right. I am," Cooper said.

Veronica and Brendan shared a look. He gave her a shrug. She sighed deeply then said calmly, "Go find it and throw it into the sea."

"Hooyah," Brendan said. Orders. He was out the door.

Jane found the strength to sit up. She searched for the Colt but couldn't find it. Veronica stood by the door for a moment as if considering what to do next. Jane could see Veronica's jaw was clinched in anger and she was pretty sure she was whispering to herself, weighing options. It was strange, obsessive compulsive behavior. This was a self-reflective moment, something she'd never seen in Veronica before.

Then Veronica took a deep breath and seemingly pulled herself together. She considered Cooper and drew the diving knife from the sheath on her leg. She said, "It's about time we break it off, once and for all." With that Veronica kneeled down and slashed his throat.

Jane screamed.

Cooper struggled, helplessly reaching up to Veronica to defend himself. Jane screamed again followed by the sound of the handcuffs ratcheting. Veronica pulled back from Cooper in confusion. In his last breath he had cuffed himself to her. Jane realized the handcuffs were in the front pocket of the fleece pullover.

It was Cooper's final act of defiance.

Veronica yanked, but she was anchored to him, and Cooper was barely alive. She cursed and tried to use the diving knife to slash his arm off. He struggled and blood sprayed her. She stabbed him more, then went back to his arm. The knife clearly could not cut through the bones in his forearm. She was now shackled and covered in blood.

"Mom?"

Veronica turned to see her son Billy standing in the shadows, the look of terror on his face.

"I told you to stay put!" she barked.

The boy had witnessed it all.

CHAPTER 21

Anchored by Cooper, Veronica shouted, "Billy, get the gun!" pointing to the Colt at his feet.

The boy hesitated.

Finally Jane saw where her gun had gone. She tried to stand but fell. The concussion was affecting her balance. Jane crawled towards the gun, and Veronica yanked Cooper, both of their progress slow.

"Give Mommy the gun, Billy. Now!"

Jane could see the boy still processing what he had just witnessed, tears streaming down his face.

"Billy..." Veronica used both hands to pull Cooper across the floor. She was making progress, and would get there quicker than Jane. Finally the boy stepped over and picked up Jane's Colt. "Shoot her!" Veronica demanded while still struggling with the single handcuff that anchored her to Cooper. "She's bad. She's going to hurt Mommy!"

Holding the pistol with both hands, a quivering Billy pointed the barrel at Jane, a look of confusion on his face.

Veronica barked, "Shoot her, Billy! Shoot her now!"

Jane tried to reason with the young mind. "No,

Billy. Killing is wrong. You'll go to hell."

"Shoot her or bring me that gun," Veronica snapped.

"Billy," Jane said, "Nobody is going to hurt you, or your mom. Go get help."

Veronica shrieked, "Bring me that gun, young man, or you're getting a very hard spanking. Do you hear me!?"

Jane could see the boy was on the fence, true fear on his face, and thought *this kid is going to need some major therapy*. Jane said, "Billy, your father needs help. We need to get him to the hospital." The boy's eyes darted to Cooper sprawled next to Veronica, his bloodied arm chained to her wrist. "Be a hero. Run as fast as you can. Get help."

"Don't listen to her," Veronica shouted.

"You hurt Dad," he said to his mother, clearly heartbroken.

"He's not your father," Veronica said.

"But he said—"

"He lied!"

"Then who is?" Billy asked.

Jane could see Billy's question threw Veronica. She said, "Your father's dead."

"Cooper is your father," Jane said. "You need to get help for him. Run!"

"Okay," Billy said, convinced it was a good idea. He stepped up to Veronica and handed her the pistol, then ran out the door of the machine shop.

"Billy! Where are you going? Get back here!" Veronica shouted.

But the boy was gone.

Jane figured she could make it and jumped to her feet. She went for the open door.

Veronica fired.

Jane's knew she'd been hit. It felt like a red hot fireplace poker had been jammed in her armpit. Her knees buckled.

This is it, Jane thought, face down on the concrete, *I'm going to die.* But then something Cooper had said, something from *The Art of War*, the idea that all warfare is based on deception.

Her idea—*play possum.*

Deception.

Play dead.

She released the tension in her body and prayed Veronica wouldn't fire again. *Let her think she won.* Other than the gunshot still ringing in her ears, it was completely silent. After a moment she heard Veronica climb to her feet. Then she heard the clink of the handcuffs and Veronica's laborious grunts struggling to drag Cooper's body across the floor. Cooper grunted. He was still alive. The next sound was a machine turning on, a low hum of some kind. The mechanical sound was familiar to Jane, but she couldn't place it.

There were more efforts, Veronica cursing with lifting weight, and then the high-pitched whine made it clear.

Jane peeked. Veronica was at the band saw. It was the same kind of contraption from high school wood shop—much like what the butcher uses to cut steaks. Veronica had hoisted him up and had Cooper's arm draped over the table. Cooper was still conscious as she began to cut his arm off at the elbow. He screamed, squirmed and flailed about.

Veronica was successful and one-armed Cooper flopped to the concrete, his neck crimson red and his arm a stub above the elbow.

Meanwhile Veronica was trying to yank Cooper's severed arm out of the dangling handcuff. But his forearm was too thick. Neither Cooper's hand nor his meaty arm could fit through the opening of the cuffs.

Veronica went back to the saw, turned it on again and was preparing for a second cut when the sound of gunfire distracted her. Still bound to Cooper's forearm, dangling at her side, Veronica went to the door to investigate. She was only a few feet from Jane.

Play dead.

For a moment all Jane could hear was Veronica's labored breathing before the distant gunfire resumed.

Cooper was still moving, so Veronica returned to him and found a crowbar. She finished him off with violent blows to the head. His skull bobbed up and down off the concrete. Jane heard the crunch and was struck with pure terror. Even if she wanted to move, Jane was frozen. *I'm truly in hell. This is evil incarnate.* Jane had been stabbed, strangled, bludgeoned, and now shot. *Is this how it ends? Does Veronica win?*

Jane remained still. *Play dead.*

She heard Veronica approach and was certain she was about to get the same crowbar treatment but then a distressed Billy cried out from somewhere in the distance, "I want my mommy!"

The blow from the crowbar never came.

Instead, as if pulled by her maternal instincts, Veronica stepped over Jane and went out the door to attend to her son.

Mommy bear's cub needed help.

CHAPTER 22

When she knew Veronica was gone, Jane reached around to feel where the bullet had entered. The puncture was under her armpit and hurt like hell. She could feel the warmth of her blood and hoped the bullet hadn't hit vital organs. Maybe she was lucky. It seemed high enough on her torso. She could still move her arm.

Jane realized if she remained there she'd surely bleed to death. She struggled to her feet and went to Cooper. His face was a concave mess—once handsome good-looks gone forever. He was the man she had loved. He was the father of Veronica's child. How could she have done this to him? So brutal.

Out the door Jane could see Veronica moving towards the cliffs. *Is she trying to get back to the yacht?* A helicopter appeared in the sky, hovering over the water. *Does she think she's getting away?*

Jane staggered out of the machine shop.

By the time Jane crossed the train tracks the Air Force Security Forces had converged—a brigade of soldiers with assault rifles. A few of Veronica's men fired back but they were cut down, no match for the professionals. But somehow Veronica walked through it all, unfazed, as if she was completely unaware of the firefight surrounding her.

Hunched low, Jane kept following, holding her bloodied hand against the seeping wound in a feeble attempt to stop the bleeding. When Veronica reached the end of the cliff she turned back, looking for Billy, presumably, but was taken aback by the sight of Jane.

Jane just stared at her, hatred in her eyes.

Veronica shouted, "How does an utter nobody like you manage take everything away from me?"

"All warfare is based on deception," Jane said. "And you underestimated your opponent, bitch!"

"Not anymore," she said. Veronica aimed the Colt. But then shouts from the soldiers distracted her. There was much commotion. Jane could see Brendan standing at the stern of his yacht. He had the rocket launcher over his shoulder; not tossing it in the water as instructed, but rather aiming it to the sky.

Veronica saw him too.

Jane's thought at that moment was simply *don't* before she saw a wisp of white smoke. The projectile banked towards the helicopter. It exploded in a ball of fire. Debris flew in every direction. The aircraft crashed into the ocean in a massive ball of flame.

Brendan thrusted his fist in the air.

The Air Force Security Forces retaliated with the .50 caliber firepower.

Brendan was cut down in an instant, and his luxury yacht destroyed. The white, fiberglass hull was ripped to shreds as if it were a Styrofoam cooler. Pieces went flying. The gunners continued to unload, ripping the boat apart until a commander screamed, "Cease fire!"

Then silence.

Jane saw Veronica drop the Colt and hold her arms up in surrender. As the soldiers closed in, she backed up against the cliff.

From the look on Veronica's face Jane knew exactly what she had in mind. Veronica took a deep breath then, as if at the edge of a diving platform, she threw her arms out and leaped backward.

Jane lost sight of Veronica over the cliff but heard her body hit with a thud. She went to the edge.

Veronica was splayed out on the jagged rocks, arms stretched out, her head bent grotesquely to its side.

Jane watched from above. She expected the master of deception to get up. Veronica always had before.

Cheat death. Let's see you do it.

Veronica moved no more.

Jane decided she'd been there long enough.

It had been four days since she'd been admitted to the Lompoc Valley Medical Center to treat her gunshot trauma and concussion. Nancy and Danny had been there, and Avery flew in from Florida to defend her. She'd given her statement, and Avery made the case for her innocence, but there was still Air Force security stationed outside her door.

She hated hospitals and wanted out. She told the doctors she felt fine, but they insisted on playing it safe. It was when they were describing her next battery of tests that she planned her escape. The challenge was to get past the Air Force guy.

The smoking section in the courtyard gave her an idea. From her window she occasionally saw patients, wearing bathrobes and gowns, go out for a cigarette. Jane didn't smoke, but the guy outside her door didn't know that.

She'd bummed a cigarette from Danny to use as a prop, and when the time was right, Jane unhooked herself from the IV and got dressed. The flimsy bathrobe her mother brought covered Jane's street clothes just enough. Showing the cigarette to the security guard, he gave her a nod and she took the elevator to the first floor.

Her deception worked.

There was an old guy she recognized, a regular in the smoking section. He had a lighter in one hand and was searching planters for a butt. Jane figured either he was out, or someone was rationing his smokes. When she approached he stepped away from the planter and gave her a smile. "Can I trouble you for a smoke, little lady?" he said.

"Sure," Jane said and gave him her Marlboro prop.

When she felt the coast was clear, Jane removed her bathrobe and stuffed it into the trash container. The old man's eyes lit up and he said, "Looks like a perfectly good bathrobe to me."

"Not my style," Jane said.

She cleared the hospital grounds and walked up the avenue. She reached the commercial district and kept going.

Jane had her life back, her name back, and for the first time in what seemed like forever—the wind at her back.

ACKNOWLEDGMENTS

My love and gratitude to my beautiful wife Jennifer whose support, great ideas, and keen instincts helped shape this trilogy. Thanks to Ricardo Netro and Peter Podgursky for creating such a cool book cover. Thanks to my supportive community of crime writer friends and filmmakers (ne'er-do-wells and otherwise) and thanks to Eric Campbell for bringing this trilogy of novellas to readers everywhere, and for everything he does with Down & Out Books.

John Shepphird is a Shamus Award winning author and writer/director of television films. He lives with his family in Southern California.

http://www.johnshepphird.com/

OTHER TITLES FROM DOWN AND OUT BOOKS

See www.DownAndOutBooks.com for complete list

By J.L. Abramo
Catching Water in a Net
Clutching at Straws
Counting to Infinity
Gravesend
Chasing Charlie Chan
Circling the Runway
Brooklyn Justice

By Trey R. Barker
2,000 Miles to Open Road
Road Gig: A Novella
Exit Blood
Death is Not Forever
No Harder Prison

By Richard Barre
The Innocents
Bearing Secrets
Christmas Stories
The Ghosts of Morning
Blackheart Highway
Burning Moon
Echo Bay
Lost

By Eric Beetner (editor)
Unloaded

By Eric Beetner and JB Kohl
Over Their Heads

By Eric Beetner and Frank Scalise
The Backlist
The Shortlist

By G.J. Brown
Falling

By Rob Brunet
Stinking Rich

By Jen Conley
Cannibals

By Tom Crowley
Vipers Tail
Murder in the Slaughterhouse

By Frank De Blase
Pine Box for a Pin-Up
Busted Valentines and Other Dark Delights
A Cougar's Kiss

By Les Edgerton
The Genuine, Imitation, Plastic Kidnapping

By Jack Getze
Big Numbers
Big Money
Big Mojo
Big Shoes

By Richard Godwin
Wrong Crowd
Buffalo and Sour Mash (*)

By Greg Herren (editor)
Blood on the Bayou: Bouchercon Anthology 2016

(*)—Coming Soon

OTHER TITLES FROM DOWN AND OUT BOOKS

See www.DownAndOutBooks.com for complete list

By Jeffery Hess
Beachhead

By Matt Hilton
No Going Back
Rules of Honor
The Lawless Kind
The Devil's Anvil

By Jerry Kennealy
Screen Test

By Ross Klavan, Tim O'Mara
And Charles Salzberg
Triple Shot

By S.W. Lauden
Crosswise

By Andrew McAleer and
Paul D. Marks (editors)
Coast to Coast vol. 1
Coast to Coast vol. 2

By Terrence McCauley
The Devil Dogs of Belleau Wood

By Bill Moody
Czechmate
The Man in Red Square
Solo Hand
The Death of a Tenor Man
The Sound of the Trumpet
Bird Lives!

By Gary Phillips
The Perpetrators
Scoundrels (Editor)
Treacherous
3 the Hard Way

By Tom Pitts
Hustle

By Robert J. Randisi
Upon My Soul
Souls of the Dead
Envy the Dead (*)

By Ryan Sayles
The Subtle Art of Brutality
Warpath

By John Shepphird
The Shill
Kill the Shill
Beware the Shill

By Ian Thurman
Grand Trunk and Shearer

James R. Tuck (editor)
Mama Tried vol. 1
Mama Tried vol. 2

By Lono Waiwaiole
Wiley's Lament
Wiley's Shuffle
Wiley's Refrain
Dark Paradise
Leon's Legacy (*)

(*)—Coming Soon

95492058R00107

Made in the USA
Columbia, SC
10 May 2018